Darkness fell as Hercules moved through the swamp. Huge snakes and rats darted around his feet. The smell of rotten eggs was overpowering. Ahead, he heard a strange, heavy panting noise as the Hydra forced its way through a thicket of trees.

The monster had nine long snakelike necks sticking out of its thick, muscular body. On the end of each neck was a square, green-eyed, sharp-toothed head. Each head was framed by a hideous mane of leathery skin and bone. All nine heads darted about the dark swamp, hissing and spitting venom.

Quickly, Hercules planned his attack. He would chop off the Hydra's heads, one at a time, from left to right.

Hercules drew near the monster. One of its heads turned, locking its green eyes on Hercules. The hero froze, waiting for the Hydra's attack. The head darted in for the kill, its jaws gaping. Its foul breath enveloped Hercules like a fog...

THE ADVENTURES OF
HERCULES

To Justin and Zach,
who like a good story

A BULLSEYE BOOK PUBLISHED BY RANDOM HOUSE, INC.

Library of Congress Cataloging-in-Publication Data:
Conklin, Thomas, 1960–
    The adventures of Hercules / Thomas Conklin.
        p. cm.
    "A Bullseye book"– T.p. verso.
    Summary: Retells the Greek myth of the great hero who must
tackle twelve impossible labors to clear his name of a deadly crime.
    ISBN 0-679-88263-4 (pbk.)
    1. Heracles (Greek mythology)–Juvenile literature. [1. Heracles
(Greek mythology) 2. Mythology, Greek.] I. Title.
    BL820.H5C66 1996
    398.2'0938'02–dc20   96-17022

RL: 5.7

Printed in the United States of America 10 9 8 7 6 5 4 3 2 1

THE ADVENTURES OF
HERCULES

by Thomas Conklin

BULLSEYE BOOKS

Random House 🏠 New York

ABOUT THE NAMES
IN THIS STORY

The Adventures of Hercules is based on myths that
are thousands of years old. Ancient Greeks and
Romans told stories, or myths, for many reasons.
Sometimes myths conveyed religious messages.
Sometimes they explained the way nature
worked. Sometimes myths were told just for
entertainment.

The greatest hero of these myths was known
by many names. The Greeks called him Heracles.
The Romans called him Hercules. This book con-
tains the most commonly used names of mytho-
logical characters and places. All of the names
listed are Greek, except for the Roman name
Hercules.

PROLOGUE

Hisssssssssssssssssssssss.

The beautiful mortal Alcmena woke with a start. She sat up in bed, straining to hear the noise that had interrupted her sleep.

Hisssssssssssssssssssssss.

The sound came from down the hallway… from the nursery where Iphicles and Hercules, her two infant sons, slept.

Something was very wrong. With a stifled cry, Alcmena raced from the room. Her husband, Prince Amphitryon, sleepily grabbed his sword and followed her down the hall.

Alcmena stepped into the nursery and screamed.

Their son Iphicles lay in the cradle, crying.

The other infant, Hercules, stood upright next to his brother. Hercules was laughing. In his little fists, he grasped two giant serpents, each nearly twice as long as he. The serpents' scaly bodies were wrapped around his chubby body and legs.

Hercules smiled and tied the snakes together. Their black eyes were cold and glassy. Their jaws, dripping with venom, hung open to reveal razor-sharp fangs.

The snakes were dead—strangled by young Hercules.

Hercules was half-god and half-mortal, the son of Alcmena and Zeus, king of the gods. One day, he would face the serpents again...

CHAPTER ONE

Hercules grew to be brave and powerful, with an unquenchable thirst for adventure. By the time he was eighteen, he could outrun, outbox, and out-wrestle anyone in Thebes.

Hercules' stepfather, Prince Amphitryon, taught him to master the chariot and bareback horse riding. The great hero Castor showed him the secrets of shooting arrows and throwing javelins and taught him battle strategies and ambush tactics. Soon Hercules became more skilled at the arts of war than his teachers.

Despite Hercules' love for physical activities, he also was schooled in geometry and music. To the demigod, learning math and the lyre were fates worse than death. But every afternoon, he met with Chiron, a centaur—half-horse, half-man—who taught him math, and Linus, a mean, withered old music teacher.

One bright afternoon, Hercules could not focus on his geometry lesson, no matter how hard he tried. While Chiron droned on in the cottage, Hercules' thoughts wandered outside. He day-dreamed he was a great hero. Soldiers chanted his name as they charged into battle. *Hercules! Hercules! Hercules!*

"Hercules, you are hopeless," Chiron scolded, interrupting Hercules' reverie. He tapped a finger on the side of Hercules' head. "You must pay attention."

The demigod looked sheepishly at his mentor. "Let's skip the geometry problems today, Chiron," he said. "I'd rather practice my archery. If I'm going to be a great hero, I need to practice."

"You must learn that your mind is more important than your muscles," Chiron replied. "To be a hero, you must learn that every battle is won with the head—not with weapons. You must outsmart your enemies."

Hercules' voice rose in anger. "But geometry will not help me win a battle!"

Chiron gave his student a stern look. "You are wrong. Which battle positions are the strongest? How does an army position itself in defense? It is all a question of geometry. To be a hero, you must also control your emotions. Jealousy, anger, and fear have been the downfall of many men."

Hercules started to argue with the wise old centaur, but suddenly he stopped mid-sentence.

"You are right. I am sorry for yelling at you," Hercules apologized. "My temper does get the best of me sometimes."

Chiron nodded. "Good. Understanding your anger is the first step toward defeating it. That is enough of a lecture today. Go on to your music lesson."

Hercules groaned. "Do I have to? I can't stand the teacher, Linus. He is always in a bad mood. He takes all the fun out of music."

Chiron pushed his young student to the door. "You may be the best athlete in all of Thebes, Hercules. But you need your music lessons!"

Hercules jogged from Chiron's cottage to Linus' grand house. As soon as he stepped into the doorway, Linus started to yell at him.

"You're late! We have a lot of work to do. Start playing," he ordered.

Obediently, Hercules picked up the lyre and began to play. He struggled through the first few bars and continued to pluck wrong notes all the way through to the end.

Linus was enraged. He demanded that

Hercules play the song over and over again until he got it right. After three hours of practicing, Hercules still could not get through the whole song without making a mistake.

"The lyre is a gift from the gods," Linus sneered. "It is supposed to create beautiful music. It is not a bow and arrow set. You cannot pull the strings any way you feel like it."

Hercules placed the instrument in his lap and bowed his head. "Sorry," he said meekly.

"Play the song again, Hercules," Linus commanded. "And this time, remember that we are trying to make music. Begin!"

Once more, Hercules plucked the strings of the lyre. His fingers were stiff and sore. Accidentally, he played a wrong note.

"No!" Linus yelled, and slapped Hercules sharply across his back. "Start again!"

Hercules replayed the tune and stumbled again.

"Wrong!" Linus' hand swept across Hercules' back. The blow stung. "I am prepared to stay here all night until you get it right. Play it again!" he ordered.

Hercules felt his face redden and his muscles tense. *I can't take much more of this. If Linus hits me one more time…*he thought as he started the tune from the beginning.

"No, no, no!" Linus yelled, sharply hitting Hercules with each word.

"Stop!" Hercules roared, and leaped to his feet. "Stop hitting me!"

Hercules pushed the lyre into Linus' hands. The music teacher cried out and lost his balance. He tumbled backward onto the polished marble floor.

"Linus?" Hercules asked, standing over the old man. "Linus, I am sorry I yelled at you. But you should not have hit me. Linus?"

The music teacher did not move.

"Linus?"

With panic growing in his heart, Hercules bent over his teacher. The old man's eyes stared blankly into space. His mouth hung open. A small pool of dark red blood oozed around his head.

Hercules immediately ran for help. But no one could help Linus. The fall had killed him.

Linus' death became the talk of Thebes. Everyone in Thebes knew that Linus often hit his students. But they also knew about Hercules' extraordinary strength and his quick temper. Some people thought that Linus' death wasn't an accident. They accused Hercules of killing Linus on purpose. Hercules would have to stand trial before the court of King Creon and prove that he was innocent.

On the day of the trial, Hercules and his family were taken to the royal palace. King Creon sat on his throne, surrounded by six of the oldest, wisest citizens of Thebes. Hercules' mentor, Chiron, was also beside the king.

Hercules tried to stay calm, but his heart raced and his knees were weak. He quickly told the court what had happened to Linus. As Hercules spoke, his mother, Alcmena, wept quietly. His stepfather, Amphitryon, and his brother, Iphicles, tried to comfort her.

After Hercules finished his story, the room was silent. Several minutes passed before King Creon finally spoke.

"Hercules," the king called out in a deep, majestic voice. "I have considered the evidence concerning the death of Linus, the music teacher. I have listened to what you and others have said about Linus' rough teaching methods. After much thought, I have reached a verdict. In the case of the death of Linus the musician, the land of Thebes hereby finds you not guilty."

Hercules' family sighed with relief.

King Creon peered down at Hercules, a somber expression on his face. "It is obvious that Linus' death was a terrible accident," he continued. "It is also obvious that you must learn to control your temper. Hercules, you are free to go."

Hercules bowed to the king and thanked him. "You are a fair and just ruler," he said. "I will try to live my life as you do." Then the demigod smiled and headed home to celebrate his freedom.

CHAPTER TWO

To show his appreciation and respect, Hercules volunteered his services to King Creon. More than anything else, Hercules wanted to be a warrior. As he entered King Creon's throne room, Hercules hoped that King Creon would award him a position in the royal army. He dreamed of one day leading the king's soldiers to victory.

"Hercules, I am honored to have you in my command," King Creon welcomed him. He looked at Hercules' bulging muscles and said, "You are young and strong. You will make an excellent...cowherd."

Instead of fighting on the battlefield, Hercules was sent to work on a farm several miles from the royal palace. The farm was owned by Thestius, a distant cousin of the king.

Hercules was disappointed, but he had given his word to King Creon. He accepted his new job at the farm.

Every morning, Hercules rose at dawn and herded Thestius' cattle to the beautiful mountain pastures of Cithairon. At dusk, he turned back and returned the cattle to their corral. The work was hard and the hours were long, but Hercules did not complain. He enjoyed the peaceful solitude and the strenuous exercise.

Soon I will be a great hero, Hercules vowed. He was determined to prove himself to Thestius and eventually earn a place in King Creon's army.

One day, Hercules was crossing the hills of Cithairon when a woman's scream echoed through the valley. Hercules looked out across the pasture and saw Thestius comforting his wife, Celeste.

Hercules dug his heels into his horse and galloped to meet them. "Thestius! Celeste!" Hercules called. "What's wrong?"

The old couple looked up at Hercules. Celeste was sobbing quietly, and tears stained Thestius' face.

"Istheus—" Thestius stammered.

"Istheus, your dog? What happened?" Hercules asked.

Unable to speak, Thestius pointed to the farmhouse.

Immediately, Hercules dismounted from his horse and ran into the building. On the floor, bloody and torn, lay the dead body of Istheus, Thestius' dog.

"The lion of Cithairon has returned," Thestius said, joining Hercules. "We are all in danger."

"A lion did this?" Hercules asked in amazement.

"Yes. The great lion of Cithairon terrorized the countryside long ago," explained Thestius. "No farmer dared venture out of his house for fear of the beast. Then, suddenly, the lion disappeared. We thought it had gone south to seek fresh prey. It never bothered us again…until now."

Hercules and Thestius buried Istheus' body. Then they met with all the local farmers. If they didn't take action, the lion would ruin their lives. Some men wanted to ask King Creon for help. They needed an entire army to hunt the lion. Others wanted to abandon their land. No one wanted to face the deadly beast. No mortal could defeat it.

As the debate continued, Hercules took Thestius' small bow and a few arrows. He slipped from the brightly lit farmhouse and stole into the shadowy hills above. While the others just talked about what they should do, Hercules was going to act.

Hercules shivered in the cold night air. He looked around the hillside, wondering where to search for the lion. Overhead, the stars twinkled silently. Then a bolt of lightning flashed across the black sky, illuminating a steep hill crowned by rocks.

Quickly, Hercules covered the distance to the hill and climbed up to the top. A terrible stench enveloped him as he crawled over a fallen tree and slipped in a slimy pool of muck.

Hercules looked down and gulped. He was standing in the guts of a dead steer. Its glassy black eyes stared up into his. The lion had to be close by.

It's only a lion, Hercules reasoned. *It can be killed.* He pulled an arrow from the quiver and fitted the notch against his bowstring. Peering into the darkness, Hercules quietly crept forward to a cave in the rocky wall.

A low growl rumbled ahead, and Hercules froze. A pair of pale green eyes loomed over him from the depths of the black cave. Hercules raised the bow and drew back the arrow. He steadied his trembling hand and focused his aim.

The lion sprang, and Hercules let the arrow fly. The lion's massive body fell on top of him. The demigod thrashed beneath the lion's great weight, punching its bony, iron-hard ribs. But the lion did not fight back. Confused, Hercules rolled free and stared at the big cat in the moonlight.

Hercules' arrow had lodged in the lion's gaping jaws. His shot had been perfect. The arrow had penetrated the lion's mouth and into its brain, killing the beast in mid-leap.

Hercules placed his hands on his hips and prodded the dead lion with his toe. Smiling, he raced back to the farm to tell everyone the good news. The great lion of Cithairon would trouble them no more.

CHAPTER THREE

When Hercules reached Thestius' farmhouse, the farmers were still arguing over the lion.

"Where have you been, Hercules?" Thestius asked as the demigod came in from the cold. "You shouldn't wander too far now that the lion has returned."

Hercules laughed and sat down at the table. "The lion won't be bothering you good people anymore. I've killed it with your bow and arrow."

The farmers were astounded. No mortal had ever faced the lion and lived. Hercules had saved them all.

The next day, Thestius told Hercules to return to Thebes. "A hero should be more than just a cowherd," he said. "You must talk to King Creon and join his army."

Thestius showed his thanks by giving Hercules a thick wooden club. The grateful farmers had carved it from an olive tree as a gift for their brave friend.

"It is I who should be thanking you," Hercules said, and headed down the road to Thebes.

Halfway home, Hercules stopped to rest at an inn. His throat was dry, and sweat clung to his forehead.

The inn was cool and dim inside. Three men sat at a table near the door. They turned slowly and stared at Hercules. One of the men had gray hair and a wrinkled face. His two companions were tall and powerfully built. One of them had a long scar on his cheek. The other wore an eye patch.

Hercules sat near the trio and dropped his club on the dirt floor. The men glared at the demigod, then continued their conversation.

The innkeeper walked over to Hercules' table. "What can I get for you, young man?" he asked.

"Innkeeper!" the scar-faced man roared. "More meat! Now!"

Hercules stared at the other table, then looked at the innkeeper. "Please bring me a cold drink."

The innkeeper nodded his head and disappeared into the kitchen.

"You have a lot of nerve, peasant," the one-eyed man addressed Hercules. "You should have some manners when you're with your betters."

A flash of anger shot through Hercules. He took a deep breath and smiled calmly at the men. "I *am* polite with my betters," he said. "I'm even polite with people like you."

The scar-faced man snarled and stood up, putting his hand on the sword at his side.

"Take it easy," said the gray-haired man. "Don't get distracted by this peasant. Save your anger for King Creon. This year, we are really going to make him pay."

"King Creon? What business do you have with the king?" Hercules asked, eyeing their swords.

The three men laughed wickedly. The one-eyed man shook his head at Hercules. "Stick to milking cows, or whatever it is you do, boy. Leave important business to men."

Anger surged through Hercules. "By Zeus, if you hurt the king, you'll pay with your lives!" he threatened.

"I doubt that, peasant," the gray-haired man replied. "We are ambassadors from King Erginus.

Every year, Creon pays one hundred cattle for protection against King Erginus' army. We are here to collect this year's debt. If you get in our way, you will be very sorry." The gray-haired man nodded to his companions as all three men drew their swords.

"Let's cut off his nose as a souvenir," threatened the scar-faced man.

The other two laughed. Hercules smiled, although his heart raced. "Why not take my ears, too?" he suggested.

"Not a bad idea," the scar-faced man said as he leaned over the demigod and pressed his sword against Hercules' face. Hercules felt a sting of pain and a warm trickle of blood run down his cheek.

In a split second, Hercules swung his club and knocked the legs out from under the three men. In one smooth motion, he snatched the gray-haired man's blade and held it to the man's throat. "Go back to King Erginus. Tell him that King Creon's debt has been paid in full...forever!"

The three men shrank back in fear. They agreed to Hercules' demands and fled the inn.

Hercules laughed and threw down the sword. The innkeeper brought him a drink, and he gulped it down before going out into the hot sun.

*   *   *

News of Hercules' victory over the lion of Cithairon had spread quickly to Thebes. At the royal palace, King Creon, Alcmena, Prince Amphitryon, and Chiron anxiously awaited Hercules' arrival. Sunlight streamed through a window and reflected off the decorative shields and spears that lined the walls.

Finally, Hercules strode through the palace gates. King Creon greeted him warmly.

"Welcome, Hercules," the king said. "I was pleased to hear about your triumph over the great lion of Cithairon. Killing that beast took extraordinary courage and skill."

Hercules looked up, his heart filled with pride. "In my soul, I am a warrior," he said. "Thestius sent me back in the hopes that you will allow me to join your army."

King Creon shook Hercules' hand and replied, "Yes, you will start your new position tomorrow. Our army needs you."

Suddenly, a soldier burst into the room. "King Erginus' army is on the march!" he shouted. "A man assaulted King Erginus' ambassadors at an inn, and they are coming from the south to attack Thebes!"

Hercules frowned and turned to the king. "It is my fault. Those men were insulting you. I didn't think they would attack. We must fight back."

King Creon paced nervously. "How can we fight back?" he moaned. "All of our troops are defending the far borders to the north. Erginus is attacking us from the south. We have no troops to fight with."

Hercules looked at his family and King Creon's faithful servants. They all stared at the king, anticipating the worst.

"The troops may be gone, but we have plenty of strong arms and brave hearts here," Hercules said.

"They are not soldiers. They cannot fight a brutal army—not in hand-to-hand combat. And we don't have any weapons," King Creon moaned, continuing to pace.

Hercules' eyes fell upon the shields and spears hanging on the palace walls. "Oh, yes, we do."

Quickly, Hercules gathered the townspeople together and organized a small army. He led them to the top of the mountain passage on the southern road to Thebes.

King Erginus' troops marched down the dusty road, the king's three ambassadors proudly leading the way. When they reached the mountain passage, Hercules climbed down to the road. Alone, he faced Erginus' army.

"Halt!" the scar-faced ambassador ordered. "It's the rude peasant from the inn. Kill him!"

Hercules held up his club and called out a reply: "Turn around and go back to your king and no one will get hurt."

"We are going to take over Thebes, and you will be the first one to die!" yelled the one-eyed ambassador. He drew his sword and charged at Hercules.

The demigod nimbly jumped out of the way. He quickly swung his club, knocking the sword from the man as his horse charged past. With a second flip of the club, Hercules knocked the man from the saddle.

The gray-haired ambassador watched in horror as his companion fell. Then he drew his sword and pointed it at Hercules. "Charge!" he screamed.

Hercules looked up at the mountaintop and waved his club at the townspeople. Instantly, hundreds of bronze and brass spears filled the air. They rained down on Erginus' army, hitting the soldiers as they rushed forward. Dozens of men fell dead.

As chaos and terror tore through the army, Hercules charged forward, swinging his club wildly. He waded into the front-line troops, knocking dozens of soldiers from their horses. At first, the troops tried to fight back, but then the army turned and stampeded in retreat.

In minutes, it was over. The mighty army of King Erginus was defeated, and Thebes was safe. Panting, Hercules looked to the mountaintop. The townspeople cheered and chanted Hercules' name. Their hero had come home.

CHAPTER FOUR

King Creon kept his promise, and Hercules took his place among the king's soldiers. He fearlessly led the king's troops into other battles and won many victories for Thebes.

Stories of Hercules' feats, on *and* off the battle-field, were known all over town. It seemed as if no mortal, beast, or monster could defeat the demigod.

But one woman stole his heart—Princess Megara, King Creon's daughter. Hercules and Megara were married in the royal palace. The gods looked favorably on the happy couple and blessed them with two sons.

Every day, Hercules worked side by side with King Creon's men. And every night, he and

Megara sat by the fire and told their newborn children about Hercules' triumphs.

"Tell them about the serpents again," Megara begged her husband.

"I've told this story a thousand times," Hercules said, then started the story anyway. "When I was just a child, Hera sent two serpents to kill me. Hera, my stepmother and queen of the gods, didn't want any stepchildren. She hated me."

Megara shuddered and interrupted the story. "Hera *still* hates you. You survived the serpents, and she still wants you dead. Aren't you afraid she might come after you again?"

Hercules put his arm around his wife. "Don't worry about Hera," he assured her. "She can't hurt me. I'm too strong. I'm more than a match for Hera."

Megara sighed. "I know that you can take care of yourself," she said. "But what about our sons? They're just tiny, helpless babies."

"Don't worry," Hercules said. "Hera will have to kill me before she can get to our children. I will protect us."

Hercules smiled, kissed his wife on the cheek, and headed off to bed.

That night, Hercules dreamed that he was wandering through a thick fog, searching for Megara and their sons.

"Megara?" he called out. Hercules strained his ears for her response.

Hissssssssssssssssssssssss.

"Megara?" Hercules called again and again. The fog grew thicker.

Then, through the mist, Hercules saw Megara. Her long black hair glistened in the faint light. Hercules walked up to his wife and leaned over to kiss her–but the woman wasn't Megara. Her face was deathly pale, and her large eyes glowed red.

Hercules' pulse raced. He stood face to face with Hera, queen of the gods.

"So, you are more than a match for me?" Hera sneered.

Hercules stood tall as he faced the goddess.

"Yes," he said proudly. "I'm a hero. I'm strong–even stronger than you. You couldn't kill me as a child, and you can't now."

Hera glared coldly at Hercules. "You are a fool," she said. "Up until now, I've only been toying with you, Hercules. The time has come for you to see just how dangerous I am...and just how terrible life can be."

Hera laughed wickedly. Then the queen of the gods disappeared in a blinding flash of light. Her laughter slowly faded away, replaced by a loud *hissssssssssssssssssssss.*

Hercules' dream continued, taking him back

to the night of the serpents' attack. Hercules saw the nursery, the bars of the crib, and the two huge serpents slithering across the floor toward him.

Quickly, the serpents climbed up the crib. The first one thrust its head in front of Hercules' face. Hercules tried to grab it by the throat but missed. The second serpent wrapped its body around Hercules' neck. He reached up to peel it away, and the snake's body tightened, strangling him. Hercules dug his fingers into the snake's scaly body, but it only drew its grip tighter. Hercules felt his knees buckle, then everything went black.

A terrified scream jolted Hercules from his nightmare. His wife, Megara, was standing next to their sons' cradle. Slowly, she turned and stared at him. Her eyes were filled with tears.

"Hercules," she gasped. "Hercules, what have you done?"

Megara stepped back from the crib, her eyes fixed on Hercules' face. Confused, Hercules got out of bed and peered into the crib.

Their two sons lay lifeless on the mattress. Their faces were blue, and their necks were badly bruised.

Hercules fell to the ground, weeping. His sons had been strangled to death.

"Hercules," Megara moaned again. "Hercules, what have you done?"

*   *   *

The news of the deaths quickly spread through Thebes.

Hercules' soul was wracked with guilt and grief. Unable to eat, sleep, or work, Hercules quit King Creon's army. He spent day after day wandering the town aimlessly, praying to the gods for forgiveness. It was the worst punishment any god could inflict.

With nowhere else to turn, Hercules consulted his mentor, Chiron.

"Hercules, you will not rest until you make peace with the gods. Seek guidance from the great temple of Delphi," Chiron advised. "I cannot go with you. You must face the oracle and its judgment alone. The oracle will tell you what you must do to pay penance for the death of your sons."

"I understand," Hercules said weakly. "No matter what the oracle mandates, I will do it."

Chiron smiled and shook Hercules' hand. "I believe there is greatness within you, Hercules," he said. "You will overcome this tragedy."

The next day, Hercules climbed the marble steps of the temple of Delphi. Inside, the temple was dark, except for the pale flame flickering in a silver oil lamp hung from the ceiling. Hercules peered into the shadowy corners of the temple, looking behind the massive marble pillars for the famed oracle of Delphi.

"Welcome, Hercules, son of Zeus," said a low voice. Hercules spun around. He saw no one.

"Who's there?" Hercules asked.

"Your heart is heavy, weighed down by your crime," the voice said.

Hercules stared up at the flickering flame. "I didn't kill my sons," he pleaded. "You must believe me. I didn't. I couldn't!"

The temple fell silent. Hercules could hear his own heartbeat.

"You placed yourself above the gods," the voice said at last. "You claimed that you were more powerful than Hera. She sent her snakes to prove you wrong."

Hercules hung his head in shame. "I should not have offended the gods," he said. "For that, my two innocent sons are dead. I will do anything to make it up."

The temple was silent. Then the flame in the lamp flared up, almost reaching the ceiling.

"Your punishment is clear," the oracle said. "You placed yourself above the gods. Now you will find yourself beneath the worst of men. The king of Tiryns is a mean, petty man named Eurystheus. Hercules, you must serve King Eurystheus and perform twelve labors. Once those labors are completed, you will be freed of your guilt."

Hercules looked up at the yellow flame. "I will do as you say."

The flame flared up and went out. The temple fell dark and silent.

CHAPTER FIVE

The oracle of Delphi had spoken. Hercules said a hasty good-bye to Megara and his family and traveled to Tiryns.

At the gates of King Eurystheus' palace, Hercules introduced himself to Diogenes, the king's prime minister.

"I am Hercules of Thebes," he announced. "I am here to offer my services to King Eurystheus. I will do any twelve tasks he asks of me."

Diogenes excused himself and consulted with the king. Minutes later, a dozen armed guards led Hercules to the king's throne room.

King Eurystheus was a frail man. His thin beard barely covered his chin, and his eyes were filled with fear.

"So you are the mighty Hercules," King Eurystheus greeted him weakly. "Diogenes says that you are here to help me. You headed up King Creon's army, didn't you?"

"That's right," Hercules answered.

"And now you want to be my slave." Eurystheus walked around Hercules and prodded one of Hercules' muscular arms. Then he flopped down on his golden throne. "Tell me, Hercules, why do you want to work for me?"

Hercules looked at the floor. "The oracle of Delphi ordered me to," he said. "I owe a debt to the gods. Serving you is my sentence."

Eurystheus laughed. "Well, well, well," he said. "The gods have picked me to be your punishment. That's quite an honor."

"You are supposed to give me twelve tasks," Hercules explained. "When I've done them all, I'll be free."

"Twelve tasks, huh?" Eurystheus stroked his scraggly beard. "I'm sure I can come up with a few things around here for you to do."

"Your Majesty, I'd like to make a suggestion," Diogenes cut in. "Our army needs training. Hercules could help us—"

"Nonsense!" Eurystheus sneered. "This is a rare opportunity. Hercules is a demigod. We need to give him a job that will be…challenging."

Suddenly, Eurystheus turned to Hercules. He flashed a sinister grin and said, "Hercules, I will accept your offer. You will stay here as my slave until all twelve tasks are done. Report to me tomorrow to receive your first task. I want to think about how to best use your unique talents."

"I look forward to serving you," Hercules politely replied, and left the king to his wicked schemes.

Diogenes showed Hercules to his quarters. His new home was a small room in a humble farm-house near the palace. The room was furnished with an old cot, a chair, and a small table.

It took the hero only a few moments to recover from the trip to Tiryns. After introducing himself to a few of the farm hands, he joined them in their toils. By nightfall, Hercules had done the work of ten men before he finally lay down on the cot to sleep.

In the palace, King Eurystheus listlessly paced the marble floor. He couldn't decide which labor to ask of Hercules. Eurystheus had only twelve chances, and he couldn't afford to squander any with Diogenes' silly suggestions. Yet nothing he thought of seemed difficult enough.

The dilemma had put the king in a foul mood. He did not enjoy the sumptuous dinner feast or the daily counting of his treasury. The image of Hercules plagued his mind even after he pulled back his bedcovers.

Eurystheus tossed and turned for hours. Then suddenly, he fell into a deep, magical sleep, and began to dream.

The king dreamed about a magnificent banquet hosted at Mount Olympus. The ambrosia and nectar were more delicious than anything he had ever tasted. A golden harp plucked a lulling tune.

Then suddenly, he was surrounded by hundreds of trunks filled with gold coins and glittering jewels. Eurystheus plucked the largest gem from the batch—and it changed into a hissing serpent! The king screamed and dropped the snake. He turned around. There was Hera, queen of the gods.

"Has Hercules come to you?" she demanded.

The terrified king tried to find his voice. He finally stammered, "Ah, y-yes. He is m-my servant."

"No!" Hera shouted. "He is *my* servant. The Delphic oracle told him to complete twelve tasks to atone for the deaths of his sons. You will tell him to do what *I* order. Is that clear?"

"Um, all right," Eurystheus meekly replied.

"Good. Tell Hercules to bring back the skin of the Nemean lion."

The last thing the king heard was a loud *hiss*. Then he fainted.

When King Eurystheus woke up, he felt and looked terrible. His face was pale, and his eyes had large dark circles beneath them. He wrung his hands nervously as he waited for Hercules to arrive.

By the time Hercules strode into the throne room, the king was a wreck. He circled around the demigod and muttered under his breath.

"I have decided on your first task," Eurystheus finally said. "Have you heard of the lion of Nemea?"

"Yes," Hercules replied.

"Good. Kill it and bring me its skin."

The guards stared at each other in disbelief. Diogenes looked wide-eyed at King Eurystheus. "B-b-but, Your Majesty, that's not a good idea," he sputtered.

"Why not?" Eurystheus asked angrily.

"The Nemean lion is practically immortal," Diogenes said. "It's a pet of the goddess Hera. The lion kills anything that comes near it. Its skin is so tough that no knife or arrow can pierce it. Sending Hercules to kill that lion is a death sentence. Why don't we give him a *useful* job—"

"No, I have made up my mind," Eurystheus snapped. He stood up and stared at Hercules.

"Hercules, in the name of the gods, I order you to bring me the skin of the Nemean lion!"

Hercules bowed low. "Your wish is my command, sir," he said, and set off for his first labor.

CHAPTER SIX

It took Hercules a few days to get to Nemea. The land was gray and covered with bare bushes. Enormous boulders on the hillside overlooked the dusty road. The only living creature Hercules saw was a huge vulture circling in the sky above him.

"Don't get your hopes up," Hercules called to the vulture. He hoisted his club over one shoulder and repositioned the bow and quiver of arrows on his back. A bronze sword hung from his belt. Hercules was ready to face Hera's lion—if only he could find it.

Hercules prowled through the hills of Nemea for two days without seeing the lion. In fact, he didn't see any creatures at all except vultures. The country appeared to be deserted.

On the third day of the hunt, Hercules was beginning to lose hope. It would be hard enough to kill the lion once he found it. But if he couldn't find it, then his first task would be impossible to complete.

Off in the distance, Hercules spotted Mount Tretus. With renewed energy, he charged ahead to the foot of the mountain.

As Hercules scaled Mount Tretus, the landscape grew bleaker. The few growing bushes gave way to rocks and bleached bones, and Hercules noticed a stench in the air. A black cave loomed about a quarter mile away.

Hercules' blood ran cold as a ferocious lion's roar shattered the silence. Hercules jumped behind a boulder, taking cover. Moments later, he saw the Nemean lion.

It approached from the north. Hercules gasped as it drew near, heading for its cave. Nothing Hercules had heard prepared him for the sight of the beast. The lion was massive. As it trotted past, Hercules could see its powerful muscles outlined under its dark brown hide.

The lion carried a large deer in its jaws. Blood dripped from the deer's antlers and a huge wound in its throat. Flies buzzed around the lion as it made its way home.

This is my chance, Hercules thought, taking hold

of his bow. He drew his largest arrow from the quiver and placed it against the bowstring. The arrow was as thick as a broomstick and was tipped with a razor-sharp bronze arrowhead.

Hercules drew the arrow back and aimed it squarely at the lion's heart.

P////////////t!

The arrow smashed into the lion's side and splintered into a dozen pieces. The lion stopped in its tracks and dropped its prey. It turned in Hercules' direction and then slowly sat back on its mighty haunches.

Did I hurt it? Hercules hoped.

His heart fell as the lion began scratching its side with a giant rear paw. It was completely unharmed.

Next, Hercules grabbed a sleek arrow from the quiver. He drew it back and aimed for the lion's ear, hoping to send the arrow into the beast's brain.

P////////////t!

The arrow bounced off the lion's skull and rattled into the rocks behind it. The lion stopped scratching and shook its head, snapping its bloody jaws at the flies buzzing around its mane.

Looks like the arrows won't work, Hercules thought. *Time for a new tactic.* Hercules lifted his sword in his right hand and took his club in his left hand. He left his hiding place behind the rock and quietly crept up to the lion, which had resumed scratching itself.

Hercules lifted his sword and brought its razor-sharp blade down on the lion's backbone.

Clang!

The sword bent and twisted in his hand.

"Oww!" Hercules yelped, dropping the sword and shaking his wrist.

The lion turned around. Spying Hercules, it opened its mouth and bared its enormous yellow teeth. The lion snarled, ready to pounce.

Hercules lifted his club and brought it down squarely on the lion's nose.

Smash!

The club cracked against the lion's muzzle, splintering into pieces. Hercules looked down at the club's broken handle. The lion staggered back, shook its head, and sneezed.

This is ridiculous, Hercules thought, tossing aside the broken club. *I've got no more weapons. There's only one thing left to do.*

In one smooth motion, Hercules leaped upon the lion's back, as if mounting a horse. The beast roared and reared back onto its hind legs, trying to shake Hercules off. Hercules held on and wrapped his arms around the lion's neck, burying his face in its dirty black mane. The lion bounded forward, and Hercules fought to keep his balance. He reached as far as he could around the lion's neck. He managed to lock hands in front of the lion's throat.

The Nemean lion dropped to its side and rolled onto its back, trying to crush Hercules, but the demigod drew his grip even tighter. The lion gagged and thrashed violently, trying to scrape Hercules from its back. Hercules held on.

The lion wrenched left and right for several minutes before it stopped moving. Hercules pulled against the lion's neck until the beast fell limp in his arms. Finally, he loosened his hold. Hercules staggered to his feet, panting.

The lion was dead. Hercules had strangled it with his bare hands.

He stared up into the sky. "Sorry about that, Hera," he said, and gazed back down at the Nemean lion.

Eurystheus dozed on his throne. It was another long, slow, boring day in the palace, and he was in the middle of his morning nap.

Something swished under Eurystheus' nose. Annoyed, the king swatted it away and opened a lazy eye. Then he screamed.

In front of his face was the Nemean lion!

"Help! Help! Save me!" Eurystheus screamed. He scrambled up on top of his throne. The lion began to laugh.

"Relax," Hercules said, and rolled out from under the lion skin. "It's just me, Hercules. And here is the skin of the Nemean lion, just as you ordered. But the task wasn't easy."

"No?" King Eurystheus replied, still trembling on top of the throne.

"I had a lot of trouble getting the skin off the beast. My knife wouldn't cut it. Finally I had to gouge out one of its own claws and use it as a knife."

"Spare me the details," Eurystheus said, turning pale. "Just get it out of here."

"Don't worry. It's dead," Hercules replied.

"I can see that," Eurystheus snapped. "I...I just don't like its stench. So get rid of it."

"Do you mind if I keep it?"

"Why would you want to keep that smelly thing?"

Hercules lifted the skin and used its head as a hood. He wrapped the front paws around his shoulders and grinned at the king. "This thing is arrow-proof and sword-proof, and will keep me warm in the winter," Hercules explained.

"Fine!" Eurystheus decided. "Keep it! Just get it out of my sight."

Hercules bowed to the king and turned to leave. "Thanks," he said. "I'll come back for my next assignment tomorrow."

"Yes," Eurystheus called after him. "Rest assured that your next task will be much more difficult."

CHAPTER SEVEN

Hercules returned home, dead tired. He tossed his new lion-skin cloak into a corner and lay down on the cot. He closed his eyes and was just about to drift off to sleep when the door to his room creaked open. Hercules waited until he heard the door close. In a flash, he sat up, knife in hand, ready to throw it and skewer the intruder.

A young boy stood near the door. He flinched at the sight of Hercules' knife.

"Iolaos?" Hercules asked, not believing his eyes.

"Yes, it's me, your nephew Iolaos," the boy said.

Hercules lowered the knife. "Iolaos! What are you doing here?"

"I left home," Iolaos explained.

"What?" Hercules asked. "Why?"

"Why do you think? Thebes is boring. Chiron and his geometry lessons are driving me nuts. I'm old enough to help you on your adventures."

"Does your father know where you are?"

"No, but—"

"Great. This is just what I need." Hercules shook his head. "You're going straight back to Thebes, Iolaos. Iphicles and your mother must be worried sick over you."

"I don't care! I want to be a hero, like you."

Hercules looked at the boy's skinny arms and legs and smiled. "Sure you do. But first you have to finish school. And then you'll have to put a little more meat on those bones before you can tackle monsters or armies."

"But—"

"No 'buts,'" Hercules scolded. "I am glad to see you. But you're heading back to Thebes before I start my second task for Eurystheus. Now, tell me about your family."

Iolaos filled Hercules in on what was happening in Thebes. After Hercules heard that Megara and King Creon were doing well, he and Iolaos settled in for the night.

The next day, Hercules received his second

assignment from King Eurystheus: to kill one of the earth's most deadly monsters, the Hydra.

According to the rumors, the Hydra lived in a poisonous, overgrown swamp in Lerna. The Hydra nested in a massive patch of trees in the heart of the swamp. No one knew what it looked like. No one who had encountered the monster had lived to tell the tale.

As Hercules packed his weapons for the trip, Iolaos continued his campaign.

"I can help you with the Hydra," Iolaos told his uncle bravely.

"Iolaos, I told you to go home! I've got enough to worry about without you getting in my way," Hercules said, loading a large bucket of tar into a chariot.

Next to the tar, Hercules placed a quiver filled with dozens of arrows. He also put in a new club, a freshly sharpened sword, and a pair of massive bows. Then the mighty demigod tied the weapons down and covered them with a tarp.

"There," Hercules said. "Now I'm ready to tackle the Hydra." He turned to Iolaos, who sat pouting nearby. "As for you, young man, you're heading back to Thebes."

Despite his nephew's pleas, Hercules hugged Iolaos and sent him on his way. Then he hitched a horse to his chariot and headed down the road to Lerna.

Hercules stopped to rest late in the day. He could see a dark sky off on the horizon. He was close to the Hydra's swamp.

Hercules sat under a tree to plan his attack. First, he would use the bucket of tar to coat his arrows. Then he would light them and shoot flaming arrows into the trees where the Hydra made its nest. The flames would drive the beast into the open. When the Hydra appeared…then what?

Hercules had no idea what the Hydra looked like, or what its weaknesses were. He would probably have to attack it with his sword and club. But how would he kill it?

"Achoo!"

Hercules looked up, startled. The sound had come from the chariot! Hercules walked over to the back of the cart. A strange lump protruded under the tarp. Hercules drew his sword and gently jabbed at it.

"Owww!"

Hercules cut the ropes and threw back the tarp. Huddled next to the bucket of tar was Iolaos. He smiled feebly at Hercules.

"I thought I told you to go back home!" Hercules roared.

"But I can help you!" Iolaos said. "I can hand you arrows. Or I can carry your sword. Or I can—"

Suddenly, an eerie squeal rose from the swamp in the distance. Iolaos and Hercules looked over the horizon at the darkness gathering over the swamp. Iolaos gulped.

"It's too late to bring you back," Hercules said grudgingly. "Just stay out of the way. I've got a feeling the Hydra is going to be a handful."

Iolaos agreed to follow his uncle's orders. Hercules gathered up his weapons and instructed his nephew to stay with the chariot. Then he entered the swamp on foot.

Darkness fell as Hercules moved through the swamp. Huge snakes and rats darted around his feet. A putrid smell like rotten eggs hung in the air.

As Hercules moved farther into the swamp, the ground grew softer and muddier. Soon Hercules sank up to his knees with each step. Ahead of him loomed the gnarled mass of trees where the Hydra lived. A strange, heavy panting noise came from within the thicket of trees.

"I hope this thing smells worse than it fights," Hercules muttered to himself. He set down the bucket of tar and stuck a bunch of arrows into the thick black muck. Then he grabbed a nearby stick, poked one end in the tar, and using a flint, struck a spark. The stick began to burn with a bright orange flame. Hercules propped the torch in the mud next to him and pulled an arrow from the tar bucket. He lit the tar-covered arrow, notched it against his bowstring, and took aim at the trees.

"Take that, Hydra!" Hercules shouted, and let the flaming arrow fly. It arced like a comet through the dark sky and landed in the heart of the trees.

The Hydra screamed with pain. Hercules quickly lit more arrows and sent them flying into the trees. Soon the entire nest was on fire, and huge columns of orange flames shot into the night sky. Hercules stepped back, blocking his face from the heat and sparks of the raging fire.

"Nice going!" Iolaos cheered from the edge of the swamp.

Hercules turned around and called back, "I told you to stay with the chariot. Go back where it's safe, Iolaos!"

"Don't worry," Iolaos said, pointing at the growing inferno. "You've already killed the Hydra! Nothing could survive that fire! Nothing could... could...uh-oh!"

Hercules turned back to face the blaze. The Hydra was forcing its way through the burning trees. Hercules gasped. The monster was even bigger than the Nemean lion. It had nine long snakelike necks sticking out of its thick, muscular body. On the end of each neck was a square, green-eyed, sharp-toothed head. Each head was framed by a hideous mane of leathery skin and bone. All nine heads darted about the dark swamp, hissing and spitting venom.

"I've got news for you, Iolaos," Hercules said, and removed his sword from its sheath. "Something did survive. And it is definitely *angry!* Now get back to the chariot!"

Hercules waded around to the left of the Hydra as it lumbered forward into the swamp, hissing and squealing. Hercules quickly planned his attack. He would come at the monster from the side and chop off its heads, one at a time, from left to right.

Hercules drew near the monster. One of its heads turned, locking its green eyes on Hercules. The hero froze, waiting for the Hydra's attack. The head darted in for the kill, its jaws gaping. Its foul breath enveloped Hercules like a fog.

Hercules held his breath and jumped aside, swinging his sword at the monster's head as it darted past. The sharp metal sliced cleanly through the neck and severed the head, which plopped into the mud. The Hydra roared with pain while the injured neck flopped around in the air.

"One down," Hercules called, "eight to go!" He raised his sword to the monster's next head.

"Look out!" Iolaos screamed.

Hercules turned back to the neck he had just sliced open. The blood spurting from the stump congealed into two streams. As each stream hardened, two pairs of green eyes appeared at their tips. Then a gaping mouth formed at each tip. Where Hercules had sliced off the Hydra's head, two new ones grew back!

The two new heads lunged at Hercules and knocked him facedown into the muddy swamp. Hercules rolled over as one of the bloody, slime-covered heads swooped down, teeth flashing, ready to bite.

Hercules swung his sword and chopped off the head. Blood spurted from the neck and instantly began to spray into two new shoots.

"That's not fair!" Iolaos bravely cried, suddenly appearing at Hercules' side. He swatted the flaming torch against the Hydra's bleeding stump.

The hot tar from the flaming torch stuck to the monster's wounded neck and seared it shut. The neck thrashed through the air, then fell into the mud, dead.

"Good work, Iolaos!" Hercules called, scrambling back to his feet. He picked up his nephew and carried him back a few dozen yards, out of reach of the Hydra. As he set Iolaos down, Hercules grabbed the flaming torch from his nephew.

"Make as many of these torches as you can," Hercules panted. "I'll chop off the Hydra's heads and seal the wounds with the flaming tar. You keep bringing me torches."

"Right!" Iolaos ran back to the bucket of tar and started gathering sticks.

Hercules turned back to the Hydra, brandishing his sword in one hand and the flaming torch in the other. "All right, monster," he yelled. "Let's get this over with."

It took nearly an hour for Hercules to kill the Hydra. Finally, after he had sliced off the last head and seared the last neck wound shut, the body of the great monster shuddered and sank into the swamp.

Hercules stood beside the creature and caught his breath. Behind him, the fire raged on, filling the night air with its crackling flames.

Iolaos waded through the swamp to his uncle.

"Wow!" Iolaos exclaimed, looking at the horrid scaly body of the dead Hydra. "How many more of these labors do you have to do?"

Hercules laughed. "Only ten," he said, throwing an arm around his nephew's shoulder. "So how about it, Iolaos? Does the hero's life still look like fun to you?"

"I'm glad I could help," Iolaos said slowly as they left the flaming swamp. "But I think I need a little more training before I become a full-time hero."

CHAPTER EIGHT

Upon their return to Eurystheus' palace, Hercules asked one of the king's messengers to take Iolaos back to Thebes. This time, Hercules made sure that his nephew went home.

Inside the throne room, King Eurystheus and Diogenes were anxious to hear about Hercules' battle with the Hydra. The demigod was happy to comply.

"So a *little boy* helped you kill the monster?" Eurystheus sneered after Hercules finished his tale.

"Not just any little boy," Hercules replied. "It was my nephew Iolaos. But he didn't actually fight the monster. He just kept the torches burning for me."

"I thought you were supposed to complete these tasks *alone*," Eurystheus said bluntly.

"You asked me to kill the Hydra, and I did. It's dead. That's two labors down, and ten to go."

Eurystheus stood up and began pacing around his throne. A wicked smirk slowly formed on his skinny face. "All right, Hercules," he said. "Let's move on. We've been—I mean, I've been thinking about your next labor, the Arcadian hind."

"The *what?*" Hercules asked.

"The Arcadian hind is a beautiful snow-white deer," Diogenes explained. "Quite unique, too. Its hooves are made of brass. It can run faster than any other deer. And, although it is a female, the hind has large golden antlers. I believe it roams the fields of Greece."

Hercules hoisted his bow onto his muscular shoulders. "So you want me to track down this hind, kill it, skin it, and bring you the antlers."

"Not quite," Eurystheus said with a grin. "Killing the beast would be too easy for you. You would finish the job with one arrow. This time, I want you to bring the creature here, to my throne room, *alive*."

With his next task in hand, Hercules paid his respects to the king and left the palace. Diogenes hurried after him.

"Hercules," Diogenes called out. "I need to speak with you. It is extremely important."

Hercules set down his bow and waited for the prime minister to catch up.

"This next labor isn't as easy as it may sound," Diogenes said with concern. "There is something else about the Arcadian hind that you should know. It's a sacred pet of the goddess Artemis."

"So?"

"If anyone harms that hind, Artemis will be furious." Diogenes shook his head and frowned. "Artemis is a lot more dangerous than a hundred Hydras could ever be."

"I have no intention of hurting the hind," assured Hercules. "Eurystheus only wants me to bring it to him, and that's what I plan to do." The demigod patted the worried prime minister on the back and strode down the dirt road.

For days, Hercules walked the countryside searching for the hind. When he finally did catch a glimpse of the swift deer's brass hooves, he ran after the animal, chasing it through villages, valleys, and meadows. The days quickly turned into months, and Hercules did not waver from the hind's trail. He hoped that the hind would tire out before he did.

At a babbling brook, the hind's tracks led to a

shady forest. Hercules quickly darted into the woods after it, keeping his eyes focused on the deer's small hoofprints among the soft pine needles.

As Hercules ran deeper into the forest, the hind's footprints became closer together. The animal was slowing down. Soon the tracks were separated by only a few feet. Hercules stared into the brush ahead, hoping to see the hind at rest.

In the distance was a clearing, bathed in brilliant white sunshine. The thick bushes around the area were laced with white, purple, and yellow wildflowers. A single apple tree stood in the center. Sleeping at the base of the tree was the white hind. Its golden antlers glinted in the sunlight.

Hercules crept silently into the clearing. The hind stirred and opened its peaceful brown eyes.

"Are you as tired as I am?" Hercules asked gently.

The beautiful hind nodded its head.

"I have an idea. I'll *carry* you back to King Eurystheus. Then I'll set you free. Deal?"

The hind stood up. Hercules braced to sprint after it. But instead of running away, the hind trotted over to Hercules, its brass hooves clattering softly on the ground. Hercules smiled and reached out to caress the deer's snow-white muzzle. The hind tilted back its head and gently licked Hercules' hand.

"I'll try not to hurt you," Hercules promised, and picked up the deer.

As soon as the animal was in his arms, a young woman's voice bellowed, "Who are you?"

Hercules looked around nervously. The forest was dark, and the cool air was filled with the scent of wildflowers.

"Who are you?" the voice demanded. "And why are you hunting my sacred pet?"

"Goddess Artemis, have pity on me," Hercules pleaded. "My name is Hercules, and I am just a man trying to keep the gods happy."

"You want to keep the gods happy?" Artemis asked. "What do you think *I* am? Why have you spent the past year chasing my deer?"

"I'm sorry, but the gods have asked me to complete twelve tasks for King Eurystheus," Hercules explained. "He ordered me to borrow your pet. I've done my best not to hurt it."

At that, the goddess fell silent. "Hercules," she said at last. "You're one of Zeus' half-mortal sons. Out of respect for Zeus, I will allow you to take my hind. But if any harm comes to it…"

"I'll protect this deer with my life," Hercules vowed. He carried the hind out of the forest and started the long journey home.

CHAPTER NINE

For Hercules' fourth labor, King Eurystheus asked him to catch the Erymanthian boar. Again, he was told to bring the animal to the palace alive.

The boar was an enormous creature that had killed dozens of hunters over the years. It had a broad, barrel-like body and short, stumpy legs. Its fur was coarse and bristly, and the boar's ugly face was framed by two sharp yellow tusks that curled up from its lower lip.

Confidence surged through Hercules as he tracked the boar. The boar was not an intelligent animal, and the hero thought that catching it would be easy. But Hercules soon discovered that his fourth chore was much harder than it first appeared.

The boar was not as fast as the Arcadian hind, but it was much nastier. And it did not want to be caught. Whenever Hercules got close to it, the boar would turn and charge at him, its jagged tusks aimed for Hercules' belly. Hercules had managed to jump out of the way a few times, sending the boar veering off into the thick, thorny underbrush at the base of Mount Pelion.

Each day, Hercules chased the boar farther and farther up the snowy mountainside. The process was tedious, but Hercules could not think of another way to catch the animal.

Grunt! Snort! Grunt!

Hercules drew his lion-skin cloak around his body and shivered. Snow fell heavily all around him as he squatted under a large pine tree. He waited for the boar to show itself again.

Finally, Hercules saw the low, broad back of the savage boar as it waded through the snow. He waited until the boar was out in the open before he jumped out from beneath the tree, blocking the path into the woods.

"It's just you and me," Hercules called out. The boar stopped and turned. It quickly scanned the mountainside and sprinted ahead, charging into the deepening snow. Hercules ran after it, yelling at the top of his lungs.

The boar grunted loudly as it plowed into a

snowdrift. It flopped around in the snow, its stubby legs unable to reach the solid ground beneath it. Hercules ran up behind the beast.

"Move it!" he shouted, clapping his hands. Panicked, the boar managed to thrash its way through the snowdrift. Hercules continued chasing it across the mountainside.

The boar landed in a deeper snowdrift. Hercules ran up behind it and swatted its rear end with his club. The boar, grunting and squirming, once more made its way through the drift.

Hercules chased the boar through the snow all afternoon. As the sun disappeared behind the mountain peak, the boar rammed into the deepest, coldest snowdrift of the day. Again, Hercules came up behind it.

"Let's go, boar! Move!" he yelled.

The boar was still. Steam rose from its sweaty, bristly back, and hot breath steamed out from its snout.

"Let's go!" Hercules said, gently smacking the boar's butt with his club. The boar grunted once, then rolled over on its side into the snowdrift. Laughing, Hercules dropped to the snow beside it. "Had enough?" he asked the boar.

The boar closed its eyes and began to snore.

After a few minutes of rest, Hercules wrapped the heavy boar in a metal net and slung it over his shoulder. Slowly, he trudged down the mountain and walked all the way back to King Eurystheus' palace.

Diogenes almost fainted when he saw Hercules at the palace gates.

"I'll see if the king is in," Diogenes said, eyeing Hercules warily. He told Hercules to wait ouside the throne room.

Hercules dropped the boar to the floor, making sure that the metal net was securely locked. The boar squealed loudly and began to thrash violently.

The door to the throne room opened. "I don't understand it," Diogenes said. "The king was here a few moments ago."

Hercules dragged the boar through the door into the throne room.

"He must have been called away on business," Diogenes explained. "I'll tell him that you returned with the boar."

"He might not believe you," Hercules said. He looked down at the squirming, snorting boar. "I'll just leave the boar here. The king will see that I brought it back alive—"

"Get it out of here!" shouted King Eurystheus.

Hercules and Diogenes turned around, but the king was nowhere to be seen.

"Get that nasty thing out of here now!"

Hercules looked at the throne and smiled. The frightened king was hiding in a huge brass vase behind the throne.

"Your wish is my command," Hercules said, bowing to the vase.

He laughed and dragged the squirming, squealing boar from the room.

CHAPTER TEN

King Eurystheus was completely humiliated. The boar had terrified him, and he had hidden from both the animal and Hercules. All the townspeople had heard about Hercules' magnificent labors, and they idolized him as a hero. Hera, on the other hand, was not pleased with Hercules' success. She was determined to saddle Hercules with the most humiliating, least heroic task she could think of.

When Hercules approached King Eurystheus for his next assignment, the king repeated Hera's latest order: to clean the manure from King Augeas' stables.

King Augeas' farm was nestled in a valley between rolling hills along the banks of the

Alpheus River. It was a huge farm that had the largest stable in all of Greece. The stable stretched an entire mile along the river and was home to thousands of cattle.

Hercules was not looking forward to the job at hand, but he had no choice but to take it. He arrived at King Augeas' farm, ready to work.

"Here you go," King Augeas said, handing Hercules a bucket and a shovel. He pointed off in the distance. "The stables start all the way down there. I reckon it will take you five or six years to clean them all."

"How long has it been since the manure was last cleaned out?" Hercules asked.

Old King Augeas scratched his head. "Let's see…thirty years? No, it was closer to forty years ago." The king shrugged his shoulders. "I guess I let it get out of hand. Thank you for volunteering to clean them out."

"I didn't volunteer," Hercules scowled, placing the shovel across his shoulder.

"Well, just don't forget to wipe your feet before coming into my palace tonight!" King Augeas warned, and went inside.

It took Hercules almost half an hour to reach the end of the stables. When he got there, he threw open the doors.

"Whoaaaaaaa!" Hercules gasped, holding the

paw of his lion-skin cloak to his nose. The stench of manure was overpowering. Hercules' eyes watered and his nose stung as he peered into the dark stables.

Beams of sunlight slanted through cracks in the wooden walls. Cattle stalls lined either side of the stables. The cows' tails lashed back and forth, swatting at the thick swarms of flies buzzing around them. In the center of the stable was a long, straight aisle of waist-high, stinking, crusty manure.

"I'll be shoveling this stuff forever!" Hercules groaned, tossing down the shovel in anger. He turned away from the stables in disgust.

Hunting down monsters and legendary beasts is one thing, Hercules thought. *A lifetime of shoveling manure is something else. This has to be the worst labor of all!*

Hercules left the stables and walked over to the nearby river. He sat on a large rock by the water and rested his chin on his fist. *If there was only an easier way,* he thought. *If only…*

Hercules squinted in the strong sunlight. He looked down at the river at his feet. Powerful cascades of water pushed their way around his ankles. The strong currents lifted loose rocks and pebbles and carried them down the riverbed.

Suddenly, Hercules had an idea.

He waded across the river and scrambled up the cliff on the other side. He walked behind a large boulder and leaned against it, pushing with all of his strength. The boulder moved, then broke away, rolling down the cliff. It landed with a splash in the middle of the river.

"Cows, you're about to get your first bath!" Hercules called out, moving to the next boulder.

Hercules pushed several boulders into the river, blocking the natural flow of water. Water swelled up behind the rocks. Soon it began to pour over the side of the riverbank.

Quickly, the demigod ran down the cliff and across the riverbed. He grabbed the shovel and dug a shallow trench to the stable door. Water from the river poured into the trench and flowed through the stable doors.

Hercules found a comfortable spot under a shady tree. He sat back and watched as the river water pushed the manure out of the stable. Soon the water flowing down the center aisle was clear and clean.

When the job was done, Hercules took his club and walked back to the dry riverbed. He knocked the boulders loose, and soon the river was flowing along its natural route again.

Hercules strolled into the stable. The stone

floor was clean and wet, and the air in the stable was sweet and pure. The cows happily swung their tails. The flies and manure were gone.

"Not a bad morning's work!" Hercules said, smacking the haunch of a cow. It turned and looked at him with a large brown eye.

Moooooooooo! the cow lowed gratefully.

CHAPTER ELEVEN

Neither King Augeas nor King Eurystheus could believe that Hercules had cleaned the stables in one single morning. But the deed was done, and Hercules was ready for his sixth task.

"Hercules, you did an excellent job of cleaning out the stables of King Augeas," Eurystheus declared. "You removed a public health menace, and I would like you to continue on this path. For your next labor, please remove the birds from the Stymphalian marsh. They have been terrorizing man and beast for decades."

"All I have to do is chase some birds out of a swamp?" Hercules asked, shrugging his shoulders. "No problem. I'll be back soon."

Hercules turned and left the throne room, whistling a happy tune. He loaded his chariot with dozens of arrows and his stoutest bow. The Stymphalian swamp was a two-day journey. He hoped he'd be back by the end of the week.

It was still daylight when Hercules drew near the Stymphalian swamp, but suddenly the sky went dark. He jerked on the reins, stopping his horse, and peered up into the sky. Swooping over-head was the largest bird Hercules had ever seen. The bird's wingspan was more than ten feet, and it was almost as long as that from its beak to its tail feathers. The bird was so big that it blotted out the sun.

"Great Zeus!" Hercules gasped in awe. The bird circled overhead twice then called out an earsplitting *caw!* Hercules covered his ears and flinched.

Pfffffft!

Hercules turned and saw a three-foot-long feather quivering in the ground next to his char-iot.

Pfffffft!

Another feather shot down from the sky and nicked Hercules' arm as it flew past. Blood seeped out from the wound.

Without waiting another moment, Hercules snatched the horse's reins, sending his chariot hurtling out from under the giant bird. Luckily, the creature didn't follow and flew away.

Minutes later, Hercules pulled his chariot up next to the Stymphalian marsh. It was a large, shallow lake covered with tall reeds. The reeds were so thick near the bank of the marsh that Hercules could not see through them. Hercules dismounted from the chariot and grabbed his bow.

I hope that bird was the biggest one, Hercules thought as he waded into the cool marsh waters. *All of the birds can't be that size. They can't be—*

Hercules gasped. He was waist-deep in the water and could now peer through the reeds. The lake was covered with birds just like the one that had attacked him. Many were even *bigger.*

The Stymphalian birds stood on long, thin legs. Their enormous bodies were covered with copper-colored feathers. Their heads were bald, purple, and ugly, with beady black eyes and long, sleek beaks that ended in a dagger-like point.

There must be a thousand of them! Hercules' heart throbbed as he took his bow from his shoulder. He notched an arrow, took aim at the bird nearest him, and then let the arrow fly.

Caw! The bird let loose an earsplitting cry, then flew straight into the air. Hercules quickly shot another arrow into the flock of birds. Then another, and another, sending more birds into the air.

The sky darkened.

Pfffffffft!

A razor-sharp feather bounced off Hercules' lion-skin cloak. Then two more rained down on him, slicing cuts on his arms as Hercules aimed another arrow.

Pfffffffft!

Pfffffffft!

One after another, copper-colored feathers fell on Hercules. He dropped his bow and bent over, pulling his cloak around him for protection. Hundreds of sharp feathers pelted his back, but none cut through the Nemean lion's skin. Temporarily defeated, Hercules hastily picked up his bow and quiver of arrows. Then he slowly waded back to the shore.

Hercules dragged himself from the marsh into the warm sunshine. The attack was over, and he bled from a dozen cuts on his arms and hands. Panting, Hercules let his cloak drop from his shoulders. It looked like a giant porcupine hide covered with copper feathers.

Hercules sat under a tree near his chariot, dead-tired. How many of the birds had he killed? One, maybe two at the very most. How many had he driven from the swamp? None at all.

Exhausted, Hercules drifted off to sleep.

Once again, Hercules' sleep led him to dream. He dreamed that he was in a beautiful open-air temple. Thick marble pillars held up the temple's golden roof. The air was thin and cool.

Sitting on a chair in the middle of the room was the most beautiful woman Hercules had ever seen. She wore a white tunic and held a golden spear. Covering her lovely red hair was a polished silver war helmet. A wise-eyed old owl sat peacefully on a wooden perch behind her.

"Hercules, do you know who I am?" the woman asked.

"You are Athena, goddess of wisdom," Hercules replied.

"Yes," Athena said with a smile. "I want to help you, Hercules. You are my half-brother. I have been following your adventures closely. So far, you have proven yourself to be brave and wise."

"I do my best," Hercules replied. "This labor, though, is my toughest challenge so far."

"I know you are having trouble," Athena said. "If you are not careful, you will be killed. I must warn you about King Eurystheus' tasks. Hera has been telling Eurystheus which labors to give you."

"Hera?" Hercules asked. "No wonder these

labors have been so dangerous. Hera wants me to die."

Athena frowned slightly. "You are matching wits with the queen of the gods herself. But I will help you, Hercules. You cannot drive away the Stymphalian birds with your arrows."

"I know," Hercules said, and sighed.

"There is one thing those birds cannot stand: noise. That's how you should attack them, Hercules. Use the rattle. Use the rattle...."

With that, the goddess faded from view.

Hercules woke up from the dream completely refreshed.

What a strange vision, he thought. *Did I really visit Athena? And what rattle was she talking about?*

Hercules sat up and squinted out from under the tree. A large copper barrel sat on the dirt road next to his chariot. Hercules scrambled to his feet and walked over to it.

The shiny copper barrel was the size of a small drum. It was filled with small stones. Hercules shook the barrel, and it made a loud, sharp, grating noise.

"Thanks, Athena!" he called out, and smiled.

Tucking the rattle under his arm, Hercules climbed a tree and perched on its uppermost branches. Looking out over the marsh, Hercules could see the Stymphalian birds spread across its surface. He lifted the rattle over his head and began to shake it. The noise was deafening. But Hercules kept shaking the rattle as hard as he could.

The giant birds started to caw. They beat their wings angrily and flew away from the marsh. The birds took off in all directions, zigzagging and fighting their way clear. A copper mass of feathers rained from the sky. The noise of the rattle was driving the birds away.

After twenty minutes, Hercules' arms were stiff and sore. He peered out over the marsh.

Below, the blue-green water was dotted with tall reeds. Frogs jumped from the bank into the peaceful lake. The Stymphalian birds were gone.

CHAPTER TWELVE

When Hercules returned to Tiryns, the king's guards would not allow him to enter the palace. Diogenes tried to explain the situation to the demigod.

"The king refuses to see you," Diogenes told Hercules.

"Why?" Hercules asked. "I've done everything he's asked. I even chased away those monster birds! Only six more labors, and I'm finished."

Diogenes leaned over to Hercules and whispered in his ear, "The king is afraid of you."

"Afraid?"

Diogenes nodded. "You're supposed to be his slave. But with every task you accomplish, you grow more famous. Meanwhile, the king is losing his people's respect."

"Well, did he at least tell you what my next labor is?" Hercules asked in annoyance.

"Have you heard of King Minos of Crete?"

Hercules scowled and nodded his head. "Of course," he said. "Minos has a bull that was a gift from Poseidon, god of the sea…I guess I'm going to Crete."

Diogenes nodded. "He wants you to bring the bull here—and he wants it alive." Diogenes frowned sadly as he closed the palace door in Hercules' face.

To get to the island of Crete, Hercules would have to take a boat across the Mediterranean Sea. He boarded a small, rugged ship that swiftly knifed its way through the crystal-blue waters. The sky was clear, and a cool sea breeze blew through the masts. Breathing the tangy salt air, Hercules felt as though he could take on a dozen of the fiercest bulls around.

After a few days at sea, the lookout in the crow's-nest called out, "Land ho!"

Hercules gazed over the water. On the horizon, he saw the chalky white shore of Crete, fringed by dark green trees.

The ship docked at the harbor of Knossos, the capital city of Crete. Hercules left the ship and walked through the busy city streets. Minos' palace was easy to find. The huge estate sat on a hill overlooking Knossos. The beautiful buildings were made of polished blue, green, and red stones.

Three heavyset guards introduced Hercules to their king. King Minos wore a gold crown, a deep purple tunic, and a silken scarlet cape. He was sitting on a golden jewel-studded throne. Minos was rumored to be the richest man in the world. To Hercules, he appeared to be just that.

But beneath the gold and gems, King Minos had a haggard, careworn face. His black hair and beard were flecked with gray, and his blue eyes were sad. He barely smiled as Hercules knelt before his throne.

"Hercules, I have heard much about you," Minos greeted him. "King Creon tells me that you are the bravest warrior in the world."

"I don't know about that, but I'm not afraid of a fight," Hercules said. "Unfortunately, sir, I no longer serve King Creon. I am here at the bidding of King Eurystheus."

"I know all about your labors," King Minos said, nodding. "Everyone does. Your legend grows with the telling. Is it true that the Hydra you killed had one hundred heads—and one of them was immortal?"

Hercules blushed and smiled. "No, sir. But it was hard enough to kill, even with only nine heads."

"Incredible," King Minos said in amazement. "So, what brings you to our island?"

"Sir, I'm here to accomplish my next labor. I have been instructed to bring back the famous bull of Crete–the gift that Poseidon gave to you."

King Minos fell silent, and his eyes gleamed.

"You could do me no greater favor than to get rid of that beast," King Minos said at last. "It is the wildest, most dangerous creature on the island. No one has managed to kill it yet. You, Hercules, are the only man who could conquer it."

"I'm afraid I can't kill it," Hercules said. "My job is to capture it alive."

King Minos stared at Hercules. He clapped his hands twice, and a dozen servants appeared from behind a curtained partition.

"Take Hercules to our finest guest rooms," the king commanded sadly. "Hercules will face the bull in the city stadium tomorrow. Make sure the royal undertaker is standing by. I'm afraid we must prepare a grand funeral for our esteemed guest, Hercules."

The servants brought Hercules to a luxurious chamber. The walls were lined with colorful paintings and murals. The large bed had satin sheets and pillows. It was a far cry from Hercules' accommodations at the farmhouse in Tiryns.

At noon the next day, Hercules was escorted from the palace by an honor guard and placed in the king's own chariot. The driver took him down the main road of the city.

Crowds of people lined the streets of Knossos, cheering the hero as he passed. Hercules smiled and waved at the people as they threw flowers in the road.

"I didn't know my fame spread to Crete," Hercules told the charioteer.

"Yes," he replied. "They all want to see the famous Hercules before he dies."

The chariot stopped outside a huge stadium. Hercules waved to the crowd and confidently walked through an archway into the stadium.

The stands were packed. King Minos sat in a box seat overlooking the center of the ring. Hercules vaulted over the tall wooden fence around the ring in the center of the stadium. A great cheer went up from the crowd. Then the crowd hushed as King Minos got to his feet and started to speak.

"Hercules, the people of Crete salute you," the king declared. "You have asked to fight the great bull that has terrorized our land. I will grant you your wish."

Then the king pointed to a large wooden gate at the far end of the stadium. "Hercules, meet your fate!"

Hercules stared at the gate. Something pounded violently on the other side. Suddenly, the wooden gate swung open, and a huge white creature strutted into the stadium.

The bull was taller than Hercules. Its eyes, hooves, and horns were jet black, but the rest of the creature was white. The bull trotted arrogantly, its head high, its tail curling back to meet its spine.

Hercules circled around the bull. It spied him out of the corner of its eye and snorted. Its left front hoof pawed at the dirt floor of the ring. Then, quick as a flash, the bull lowered its horns at Hercules and charged.

Hercules barely managed to jump aside as the bull stormed past. The crowd roared as Hercules skipped to safety. The bull slammed on the brakes, but the momentum of its charge sent the animal skidding across the ground, raising a cloud of dust.

"You can move faster than that!" Hercules taunted as the bull turned to face him, its lips curled in anger. The bull again lowered its head at Hercules and pawed the ground, snorting with fury. It charged.

Hercules waited till the last second, then grabbed the bull by the horns. The bull skidded to a stop, then threw back its head, sending Hercules flying over its back. The crowd roared as Hercules did a flip in midair and landed on his feet right behind the mighty bull.

The bull looked back over its shoulder as Hercules bowed deeply to the cheering crowd. The bull lifted its hind legs and gave Hercules a powerful kick on the rear, sending the demigod flying across the ring.

The crowd gasped as Hercules landed face-first in the dirt. He quickly jumped to his feet and turned to face the bull.

"Hercules, how can I help?" yelled Minos. "Name any weapon in my kingdom, and it's yours!"

"No weapons," Hercules called back without breaking his gaze on the bull. "I need to capture it alive!"

Out of the corner of his eye, Hercules saw the king's red cape. An idea flashed through his head.

"I'll take that cape of yours, though!" he added.

King Minos took the scarlet cape from around his shoulders and tossed it into the ring. It floated down, landing gently between Hercules and the bull. Hercules slowly reached for the cape, gathering it up to his side. The bull eyed him warily as Hercules extended the cape from his hip. The bull stared at the scarlet cape, entranced. It lowered its head, snorting and pawing the ground. Then it charged straight at the cape. Hercules easily jumped out of the way, whipping the cape up over the bull's head as it rushed past.

The crowd cheered with delight.

Hercules spun around as the bull skidded to a stop. Enraged, it turned and snorted. Hercules waved the cape in front of its face. Again, the bull pawed the ground, preparing to charge. Again, it lowered its horns and hurled itself at the cape, only to have Hercules step aside at the last second.

From his seat, King Minos watched with awe as Hercules taunted and tired his opponent.

After four hours of chasing Hercules and the cape in the hot sun, the bull had grown tired—and tame. Now it would do whatever Hercules ordered.

Hercules led the great white beast out of the stadium and down to the docks, where a ship would take them back to Tiryns. Hercules watched as the sailors gently lowered the bull into the hold of the ship.

"That was an incredible fight!" one of the crew members said, shaking Hercules' hand.

"Thanks," Hercules replied. He nodded at the bull as it disappeared beneath the decks. "He was a worthy opponent."

"Hercules, we would love to help you out on your next adventure," another sailor added. "We're tough and we're brave!"

Hercules laughed as the young sailors crowded around him, begging to take part in his next adventure.

"I'm supposed to do these labors on my own," Hercules said. "But who knows what other tasks are in store? I just might need another boat ride."

Hercules jumped on board the ship, and they all sailed back across the Mediterranean Sea.

CHAPTER THIRTEEN

Back at the palace, King Eurystheus was distraught. Hera had been tormenting his dreams every night since Hercules' arrival. Until Hercules was dead, she would not be satisfied. Yet, even after several life-threatening labors, Hercules had not even come close to being harmed. Any other mortal would have been dead by now.

"Your Majesty," Diogenes said, entering the throne room. "Hercules has returned from Crete... with the animal in question. He also has acquired a few followers–sailors, actually."

"He's got an army now?" King Eurystheus asked fearfully. "He's supposed to do these labors alone!"

"He will, sir," Diogenes said. "The sailors have

offered their services to Hercules, in the event he might need another ship."

Eurystheus stroked his beard and sighed. "Hercules *will* need a ship for this next task," he said. "He'll be traveling far away to Thrace. He will steal Diomedes' horses!"

Diogenes left the throne room and relayed the information to Hercules. Hercules and a small band of sailors set out at daybreak.

They sailed for many weeks before finally touching the shores of Thrace. It was nighttime when Hercules and two sailors, Opdian and Abderus, reached Diomedes' dark palace, which stood at the crest of a mountain miles from the sea.

"I heard that Diomedes is a cruel, powerful man. He likes to see others in pain," Opdian said in a hushed whisper.

The three looked at the black building.

"Then we can't let him find out what we're up to," Hercules said, pointing to the stables. "That's where the horses are. Let's go."

"Wait," Abderus cautioned. "They say that Diomedes' horses are man-eaters. They live on human flesh."

"Don't be stupid," Opdian retorted. "Who ever heard of man-eating *horses?*"

"Whatever they feed on, it's our job to bring them back to King Eurystheus, alive and well,"

Hercules said, ending the bickering.

Hercules and his two companions sneaked around the side of the palace to the stables. The three men hid in a clump of bushes. Peering through the gloom, Hercules saw a pair of soldiers guarding the stables. Inside, Hercules could see a knot of thick iron chains attached to a large metal trough. The horses were not in view.

"What's that next to the trough?" Abderus whispered.

"Where?" Hercules asked.

"To the right. That big white pile. It looks like…It looks like…"

Opdian gulped. "Those are human bones," he said.

"Let's not panic," Hercules warned. "Just keep your distance from the horses. They're only horses…with a big appetite."

At that moment, Diomedes staggered into the courtyard. He was tall and fat, dressed all in black. In his left hand he carried a lantern, which threw a harsh yellow light onto his puffy face. In his right hand he carried a bullwhip.

"How are my beauties tonight?" Diomedes called out.

"They are well, sir," one of the guards answered, and snapped to attention. Diomedes grunted and walked past him into the stables.

Diomedes' lantern illuminated the dark stable. Now Hercules could clearly see that the floor was littered with human skulls and bones. Four large shadowy figures moved in the corners. Diomedes looked at them and cracked his whip.

"Back! Back!" he yelled, cracking the whip into the corners of the stable. Inside, the horses whinnied and screamed with pain as Diomedes lashed the whip from side to side. "You beasts are more trouble than you're worth!" he bellowed. "Be thankful that I'm so kind to you!" He snapped the whip a dozen more times, then turned and walked away from the stable.

Hercules waited until Diomedes had disappeared into the palace. "Here's the plan," he told his two companions. "Wait one minute, then make a noise to distract the guards. Leave the rest to me." Hercules crept off into the shadows.

Abderus and Opdian waited, their hearts pounding. After a minute had gone by, Abderus cupped his hands to his mouth.

"Help! Help!" he yelled.

The two guards stepped forward and pointed their spears at the bushes where Opdian and Abderus hid. Hercules slipped behind the men and smacked their heads together. The guards fell to the ground, unconscious.

Abderus and Opdian ran from the bushes to

the stable door. They cautiously peered inside.

"Take their spears," Hercules said, nodding to the guards. "I'll get the horses."

Hercules slipped into the dim stable. He could hear heavy breathing from the four corners of the dark building. Chains clanged together as the horses' hooves gently stamped on the ground.

"It's okay," Hercules whispered gently. "I'm not going to hurt you. I'm going to set you free." Hercules stepped over the piles of bones scattered across the stable floor. He lifted the thick chains attached to the metal trough and, using all of his strength, snapped them in two.

Holding the chains in his hands, Hercules walked to the door of the stable, gently pulling the horses after him. He entered the courtyard, where Abderus and Opdian waited, spears in hand.

The four horses emerged from the dark stable into the moonlight. Hercules could hardly believe his eyes. Once, they must have been magnificent creatures. They were jet black, with long, silky manes. But the horses were terribly thin. Gaunt ribs protruded from under their black skin. Blood-shot black eyes popped from their narrow faces, and foam flecked their lips. As Hercules gently yanked their chains, the horses bared their ugly yellow teeth and blood-red gums.

Opdian stared at them. "These are beautiful animals," he said in awe. "With a little care, I'm sure they would be champions."

"Opdian, stay back," Hercules warned as the young sailor wandered near the horses. In a flash, one of the horses lunged forward, bringing its massive head down on Opdian's arm. The sailor screamed in pain as Hercules jerked the horse away. Opdian fell to the ground, holding his arm.

"It bit me!" he cried.

Abderus rushed to Opdian's side. "Holy Zeus," he gasped. The horse had bitten a large chunk of flesh from Opdian's arm.

"Let's get back to the ship," Hercules said. "I'm afraid this is going to be a long trip back to Tiryns."

Hercules led the horses across the barren black hills to the sea, where the ship was anchored. Opdian, his wounded arm wrapped in his cloak, followed behind. The first rays of dawn lit the eastern sky as the three men and the horses neared their ship.

Off in the distance, a trumpet blared from Diomedes' dark palace, and an army of soldiers mounted an attack. The theft of the horses had been discovered. Diomedes hoped to catch the thieves red-handed. They would make a tasty meal for the four beasts.

Diomedes led the soldiers down the hillside. He squeezed through a narrow passage in the rocks. His men, weighed down with armor and weapons, struggled to keep up.

Suddenly, Hercules jumped from the top of the rocks between Diomedes and the soldiers.

Diomedes pointed to Hercules. "It's one of the thieves!" he yelled. "Kill him! Kill him now!"

"Wait!" Hercules called, holding up his hand. "I was not stealing the horses," he explained to the soldiers. "I was freeing them from a horrible life."

"That's ridiculous," Diomedes sneered. "Kill him now!"

"Diomedes, you are free to take the horses back," Hercules said. "They are waiting for you on the beach. But be warned. The horses are not chained up."

Hercules snatched Diomedes' bullwhip out of his reach. "If you care for them, you won't need this."

"I am their master," Diomedes boasted. "They will obey me with or without a whip," he added, although his voice quavered with fear.

Diomedes hesitated, then headed across the sand toward the four horses. At the sight of their cruel master, the horses went wild. They reared back on their hind legs and whinnied loudly, foam spraying from their mouths.

"C-c-come with me," Diomedes ordered. He pulled two small knives from his boot. Diomedes waved the blades menacingly at the horses.

Unafraid, the horses trotted around Diomedes, surrounding him. They reared back again, and Diomedes dropped the knives. He screamed in terror as the horses closed in.

Hercules ran down to the beach to save Diomedes. But he was too late.

The soldiers threw down their weapons. "You've freed us from Diomedes' cruelty," said one. "Let us follow you, Hercules!" another shouted.

"You may follow me if you please," Hercules said. "But I am *not* free. I have four more labors to perform, and I must accomplish them without help from anyone."

Opdian and Abderus petted the horses. Now that Diomedes was dead, they were calm and tame. Opdian flinched as the horse that had bit him drew close to him. But this time the horse licked his cheek.

"I'd say this labor is over," Hercules concluded. "Let's deliver these horses to Eurystheus!"

CHAPTER FOURTEEN

For Hercules' ninth task, King Eurystheus asked the hero to sail up the Thermodon River and bring back the jeweled belt of Hippolyta, the Amazon queen.

The Amazons were a race of fierce warrior women who lived far to the east of Greece. Little was known about them, since no traveler ever dared enter their lands.

Again, Hercules journeyed by boat. He had many traveling companions. The two sailors, Opdian and Abderus, some of Diomedes' soldiers, and even his nephew Iolaos had joined him on this latest labor.

"So, how are you planning to take the belt

from Hippolyta?" Opdian asked Hercules as the boat slowly made its way upstream.

"You might have to kill her first," Iolaos suggested.

Hercules laughed. "No, Iolaos. Hippolyta is a smart, reasonable woman. I am going to politely ask her for the belt, and she will hand it over."

"Right," Abderus chimed in. "I'm sure it'll be that simple. But I'll sharpen my sword—just in case!"

Hercules stood and gazed over the prow of the ship. A line of canoes was blocking their path. Standing in the canoes were dozens of women, each armed with a bow and arrow pointed straight at the ship.

"Ahoy, there!" Hercules called.

A tall woman dressed in a tiger skin stood in the middle boat. She raised her right hand. "Drop your anchor," she commanded.

Hercules turned and nodded to his men.

"Visitors to the land of the Amazons," the woman called. "Who are you, and what do you want? State your business."

Hercules bowed. "We mean no harm. We have come from far away. My name is Hercules. I need to see your queen."

The Amazons led Hercules and his men up

the river to the harbor of Themiscyra, where they all cast anchor.

"The rest of you stay in the boat," the tiger-skinned woman said. "Hercules, follow me."

"Will you be all right, Hercules?" Opdian asked.

"Don't worry," Hercules said. "I'll be fine." He gazed out at the crowd of tall, beautiful warriors gathered around the ship. "Besides, this can't be worse than wading into a cold marsh to fight a bunch of ugly birds."

Hercules followed the women down the streets of Themiscyra. The buildings were solid yet simple, made of unpainted wood and bark. As they walked, Hercules saw hundreds of women, all of them tall and strong. They wore short tunics made of animal furs, and they each carried a deadly weapon of some sort.

Soon the group arrived at a large fort in the heart of town. The fort was protected by a high fence of tree trunks. Guards were posted at lookout towers in each corner. Their arrows were aimed at Hercules. One guard in particular looked strangely familiar. She had long black hair, pale skin, and blazing eyes. She smiled slyly at Hercules.

Hercules passed through a large courtyard to the main building at the center of the fort. He was immediately shown inside the queen's chambers.

The walls of Hippolyta's room were covered with swords, spears, and shields—trophies from the Amazon army's battle victories. Hippolyta herself sat at a massive wood desk in the center of the room, studying papers. The leader of the army walked up to her.

"This is the man who asked to see you, Your Highness," she said.

Hippolyta looked up at Hercules. Her brown hair framed her stunning face. The queen studied Hercules and stood up.

It was then that Hercules noticed Hippolyta's clothes. She was wrapped in a lion's tunic like his. But instead of a male lion's skin, Hippolyta's was the fur of a lioness. Cinched around her waist was a glittering silver belt. Gems of all colors and sizes formed an intricate design across the front and sides.

"So," Hippolyta said. "Why are you here?"

"I have to ask a favor of you, Your Majesty," Hercules said sincerely. "I need to borrow your jeweled belt. I will return it as soon as I can."

"You want my belt?" Hippolyta said with a smile. "It was given to me by my mother. It is a symbol of Amazon royalty. I have never taken it off. If you want it, you will have to fight me for it."

"That's not exactly what I had in mind,"

Hercules replied. "Isn't there another way?"

The Amazon queen picked up her battle-ax. "If you win, you can borrow the belt. But if I win…you will be sacrificed on the altar of the goddess Artemis."

Hercules thought for a moment and shrugged his shoulders. "I must borrow your belt. I don't want to fight you, but I have no choice."

Minutes later, Hercules and Queen Hippolyta were brought to a courtyard outside the palace. Hundreds of Amazons gathered to watch their queen do battle with the intruder. Hercules stood face-to-face with his opponent.

The queen stood taller than Hercules. Her lean, muscled arms held the battle-ax in a fighting stance.

Hercules and Hippolyta faced each other and bowed.

"Let the match begin!" an Amazon shouted from the crowd.

The two opponents circled each other. Neither wanted to make the first move. Then, suddenly, Hippolyta swung the ax at Hercules' head. He parried the blow and swung at her legs. Hippolyta neatly jumped over the club as it swooshed beneath her feet.

The pair fought throughout the afternoon. Neither was able to gain an advantage over the other. As soon as Hercules pinned Hippolyta, she managed to knock him off balance and roll away. Whenever Hippolyta had the upper hand, Hercules would twist free and escape.

Finally, as the shadows of evening began to fall, the pair threw down their weapons and locked arms in hand-to-hand combat. Still neither fighter could overpower the other.

Then from out of the crowd, the familiar-looking dark-haired Amazon warrior stood up. "Sisters!" she yelled. "This is a trap! Hercules is planning to kidnap our queen and kill us all!"

The Amazon women drew their weapons, ready to shoot Hercules.

Still locked in their life-and-death struggle, Hippolyta stared at Hercules. At that instant, Hercules fell flat on his back.

"You won," Hercules called out.

Hippolyta stood over Hercules, smiling. "Sisters!" she yelled, waving her ax above her head. "I have defeated this man! We are in no danger!"

The queen held her hand out to Hercules and helped him rise to his feet. Hercules scanned the crowd for the dark-haired woman. She had disappeared.

"You are indeed a skilled warrior," Queen Hippolyta said. "You deserve to live."

Hercules bowed to the Amazon queen. The warriors brought Hercules safely back to his boat, and helped the crew cast off.

That night, as the boat drifted down the river, the image of the dark-haired Amazon floated through Hercules' memory. It was the same woman he had seen in his nightmares...just before he strangled the serpents. It was...Hera! Hera had wanted the Amazons to kill him, but yet again, Hercules had foiled her plan.

Iolaos interrupted Hercules' thoughts. "Why did you *let* Queen Hippolyta win the battle?" he asked.

"Sometimes it is braver *not* to win," Hercules answered. "And smarter. See?"

The demigod smiled and proudly showed off the prize Hippolyta had given him for fighting so bravely and so well—her jewel-covered belt.

CHAPTER FIFTEEN

Hercules had barely set foot in King Eurystheus' palace when he was sent out on his tenth assignment. Hera was angrier than ever, and she and the king had quickly plotted Hercules' next "impossible" task.

This time, Hercules was instructed to bring some of Geryon's cattle back to the palace.

The hero obediently searched for Geryon throughout Greece. Hercules searched Italy, Asia Minor, and throughout the known world—without finding Geryon.

At last, Hercules found himself in the desert of northern Africa. He crossed miles and miles of hot sand. His tongue, dry and swollen, stuck to the roof of his mouth. The scorching sun beat down mercilessly on his head. The lion-skin cloak, soaked with sweat, clung to Hercules' sore, exhausted body.

In a moment of weakness, Hercules collapsed in the sand.

"Enough!" he moaned, blocking the sun's bright rays from his eyes. Delirious with thirst and exhaustion, he grabbed his bow and arrow. He rolled onto his back, took aim at the hot yellow sun, and let the arrow fly.

"Who is shooting at me?" Helios, god of the sun, called down from above.

Hercules squinted at the huge sun. "It's Hercules. My apologies," he said tiredly. "You're just too hot today."

"Well, why don't you go home?" Helios' voice boomed down.

"I didn't *choose* to be here," Hercules explained. "I'm looking for a herdsman named Geryon. I must find him and bring a few of his prize cattle back to Tiryns. I've searched everywhere. No one has even heard of Geryon. Have *you* seen Geryon?"

"I see *everyone*," the sun god replied. "Geryon lives in the north."

"Oh, no," Hercules moaned.

The sun god smiled down on him. "Hercules,

you are honoring the mandate of the oracle of Delphi. I will help you finish this labor. I will help you find Geryon."

"Yes?" croaked Hercules. "How?"

"I'll take you north. Go to the shore. You'll find a boat waiting for you. It will take you to Geryon."

"I am in your debt, Helios," Hercules said thankfully, and slowly rose to his feet. He staggered down the sand dune to the shore.

Just as Helios had promised, a boat was anchored in the surf. It was unlike any other boat Hercules had ever seen. Helios' boat was made of solid gold. It sat high on the water and its sides curved gently like a water lily.

Amazed, Hercules waded into the water and climbed aboard. The little boat bobbed and rocked under his weight. As soon as Hercules was settled in, the boat magically started to move. It skimmed briskly across the water.

For three days and nights, the boat continued across the waves. It passed through the warm waters of the Mediterranean Sea to the cold, choppy waters of the Atlantic. Then the boat turned and headed north.

Hercules huddled in the small craft and pulled his lion-skin cloak tightly around his body. The weather had turned extremely cold. The water was gray and dotted with icebergs. The shore was lined with snow-covered pine trees.

Finally, the boat washed up on an icy shore. Hercules stepped out onto land, saluted the sun with his club, and continued the search for Geryon.

The land was covered in deep snow. As Hercules walked through the pine forests, he kept his eyes open for signs of Geryon and his cattle.

At midday, Hercules came upon a dog lying peacefully at the edge of a snowy pasture. As he approached, he called out a friendly greeting to the animal.

Growling, the dog jumped to its feet and turned around. Hercules swallowed hard. The dog had two heads. It bared its two sets of sharp teeth and sprang at Hercules.

Instinctively, Hercules swung his club at the dog's snapping jaws. It fell back into a snowbank.

"Sorry about that," Hercules said, stepping through the trees into the pasture.

Dozens of large, fine rust-colored cattle grazed on the tall grass that poked through the snow. A large, burly man stood at the edge of the pasture. He was dressed in a woolly jacket and wore a horned metal helmet on his head. He held a long, crooked staff in his hand.

"Hello," Hercules called to the man. "Could you direct me to Geryon? I have a business deal to discuss with him."

The man turned and looked at Hercules suspiciously. He had a huge, bristly beard and clear blue eyes. "A deal?"

"That's right. A business deal."

The man stroked his beard and stared at Hercules. "Hmmm," he mused. "I'll tell you what. *This* is how I deal with strangers."

In a flash, the man dropped his staff, pulled a dagger from his coat, and threw it. Hercules jumped aside as the knife sliced through the air, just missing his ear.

Thwack!

The knife landed in a tree trunk behind Hercules.

Hercules frowned at the man and shook his head. "First the dog, now this," he said. "All I want to do is talk."

The man groped for the sword at his side, but Hercules tackled the man in the snow before he could retrieve the weapon. In an instant, Hercules had the man pinned. Hercules sat on his chest, holding the man's own sword to his throat.

"Let's start this conversation all over again," Hercules said politely. "What is your name?"

"Eurytion," the man snarled.

"Pleased to meet you, Eurytion. Do you know where I can find Geryon? I have a business deal to discuss with him."

"Geryon does not make deals," Eurytion spat out. "I work for Geryon. I'm his cowherd. These are his cattle."

Hercules looked around the pasture. "They are fine beasts," he said. "Only one head apiece, which is how I like them. I would like to buy a few of these cattle."

A loud voice behind Hercules bellowed, "They are not for sale!"

Hercules slowly turned around. Standing behind him was the most amazing creature he had ever seen. From the waist down, Geryon was just another giant. From the waist up, Geryon branched into three bodies. Each one was broad-shouldered and muscular, with a pair of arms holding a huge bow and arrow. Each of Geryon's three trunks was topped with an ugly head—one with a red beard, one blond, and one black. His six beady eyes stared with hatred at Hercules.

"You must be Geryon," Hercules said.

"I am. Leave my cowherd alone."

Hercules released Eurytion and stood to face Geryon. "You northerners have a strange way of welcoming strangers," Hercules said.

"We have only one way to welcome thieves

like you!" Geryon's center head said.

"What makes you think I'm a thief?" Hercules asked.

"You killed my guard dog!" Geryon snarled, pointing to the woods.

"That was your dog?" Hercules looked at Geryon's three heads. "He attacked me first."

"Of course he did!" Geryon's center head bellowed. "He was trained to attack thieves!"

"Let's kill him!" his left head said.

"Now!" the right head said.

Eurytion woozily stood up behind Hercules.

"Just calm down," Hercules said. "Get this through your head—er, heads. I am not a thief. My name is Hercules. I want to buy a few of your cattle—"

Suddenly, Eurytion grabbed Hercules, pinning his arms behind his back.

"Let's stop wasting time!" Eurytion called to Geryon. "Kill this thief now. His pretty blond scalp will make a nice pillowcase."

"Good idea!" Geryon's middle head said.

"I'll kill him!" the left head said.

"No," the right one argued. "I'll do it!"

"We'll all kill him," the center head said. "Shoot him on the count of three."

Hercules cringed as Geryon's three bodies each aimed an arrow at his heart.

"One," yelled the left head.

"Two," the right one counted.

"Three!" they all called at once.

Pffffft! Geryon's arrows flew through the air.

Hercules nimbly turned Eurytion around. The cattleherd screamed in agony as the three arrows pierced his back.

Hercules dropped Eurytion's body and sprinted to the left.

"Hey!" Geryon bellowed, looking to see where Hercules had gone. "Come back here!"

Hercules skidded to a stop alongside Geryon and drew an arrow from his quiver.

Another round of arrows flew from Geryon's bows and missed their mark again. Hercules let his single arrow fly.

The arrow sliced cleanly through Geryon's three necks, lodging in the third. The giant staggered and fell into the snow.

Hercules walked up to Geryon's body. The giant's six lifeless eyes stared up at the winter sky. "Northern hospitality," Hercules said, shaking his head as he hung his bow over his shoulder. "I'm glad I live in Greece."

The hero picked up Eurytion's staff and began herding the cattle south.

CHAPTER SIXTEEN

For the first time since Hercules had arrived in Tiryns, he felt powerless. He had just been given his eleventh labor. The task was impossible.

King Eurystheus had asked Hercules to bring him three golden apples from the enchanted Garden of the Hesperides. No mortal knew where the garden grew, and no mortal could enter the garden or take its fruit.

Hercules wandered off the palace grounds, downhearted. After all of his hard work, after all of the danger he had faced and overcome, it had come down to this. Eurystheus and Hera had given him a task that could not be completed.

The hero walked aimlessly for hours, trying to

figure out how to find the garden. At the river Eridanus, he paused and crouched by the bank. He moved his hand through the water and prayed for a miracle. He needed the help of the gods to find the garden.

The sea god Poseidon answered his prayers. He appeared before Hercules and said, "What is troubling you?"

Startled, Hercules fell back on his haunches. "I need to find the Garden of the Hesperides," Hercules explained. "It is my eleventh labor for King Eurystheus. He might as well have asked me to bring him a set of Zeus' thunderbolts."

"I cannot tell you where the garden is," Poseidon said. "But I can help you find it. The titan Atlas planted the apple tree in the Garden of the Hesperides. He can enter the garden whenever he pleases."

With renewed vigor, Hercules thanked the sea god and started off down the road to Mount Atlas.

It did not take long for Hercules to find the titan. Atlas stood at the top of the mountain, his arms spread out and his legs bent, as though he had a great burden on his back. He was three times taller than Hercules and had huge, bulging muscles.

"Hello, Atlas!" Hercules called out.

"Who are you, mortal?" Atlas asked with a grunt.

"My name is Hercules. I need you to do me a favor."

"A favor? What is it?"

"To go to the Garden of the Hesperides and bring me three of the golden apples. I need to deliver them to King Eurystheus right away."

Atlas grunted again. "Unfortunately, I can't help you, friend. I wish I could. But I cannot move from this spot."

"Why not?" Hercules asked.

"Because," Atlas snorted, "I'm holding up the sky!"

Hercules did not see anything on Atlas' large hands. But he knew he had to convince Atlas to help him. He decided to humor the dim-witted titan.

"Atlas, why don't you take a rest? I'll hold up the sky while you get me those apples," Hercules offered.

"You'd do that for me?" Atlas grunted.

Hercules smiled. "Sure, why not? I really need those apples."

"Thanks," Atlas grunted.

Hercules quickly climbed up a cliff next to Atlas.

"Hold your arms out like mine," Atlas directed.

"Like this?" Hercules asked, smiling.

"Good," Atlas said. "Ready? I'm going to shift the sky onto you now."

"Go right ahead," Hercules said. *This impossible task is turning out to be the easiest one yet!* he thought.

Atlas lowered his arms. All of a sudden, an enormous weight crushed down on Hercules' arms. He staggered and almost fell. His legs nearly buckled out from under him.

"The sky is heavier than it looks, huh?" Atlas said, smiling.

"You...weren't...kidding!" Hercules grunted as his face turned dark red.

"You wait here, and I'll go get those apples."

Hercules groaned as Atlas ambled away. The weight on his shoulders seemed to get heavier and heavier with each passing second. He was utterly paralyzed by the burden.

A few moments later, Atlas reappeared. He carried three beautiful golden apples and was grinning from ear to ear.

"Boy, does it feel good not to have all that weight on me!" Atlas exclaimed.

"You...don't...say," Hercules grunted.

"Who did you say these apples were for? King Eurystheus? I'll deliver these apples to the king myself. You're a big, strong guy. You can hold up the sky for a while."

"Are you...sure...you want...to do that?" Hercules asked.

"Certainly. Maybe I'll take a little vacation too. I've earned it."

Hercules started to panic. If Atlas left, he would be stuck here forever!

"All right, Atlas," Hercules said, finally. "Go ahead. Have fun. I'm all right. This...is...pretty easy..."

"You'll get used to it," Atlas replied.

"There's just...one...thing!" Hercules called out. "See this lion cloak I'm wearing? One of the teeth is digging into my shoulder. Would you mind holding the sky for a second while I fix it?"

"Well, okay," Atlas agreed, and stepped next to Hercules. "Just make it quick."

Hercules' body flooded with relief as Atlas lifted the burden off his shoulders.

"Thanks, Atlas!" Hercules cried, rolling his shoulders. He jumped down from the cliff. "I'll be taking these apples to King Eurystheus after all."

"Hey, wait a second!" Atlas said. "You tricked me."

"I'm sorry," Hercules said, picking up the three golden apples. "I have to go. I still owe the king one last labor!"

CHAPTER SEVENTEEN

Hercules and his friends threw a celebration for the completion of eleven of Eurystheus' twelve labors. The hero had only one task left before he was free.

The festivities were in full swing when Hercules heard a familiar *clip-clop* on the court-yard pavement. Chiron the centaur, Hercules' old friend, had come to visit.

"Chiron!" Hercules called, jumping to his feet. He ran to his old mentor and threw his arms around him.

"How are you?" Hercules asked. "It's been years since I saw you."

"I am well, Hercules," Chiron said. "Much better now that I have seen you with my own eyes. We have heard so much about your adventures."

Hercules looked into his friend's eyes. "How are Mother and Amphitryon? And...and Megara? How is she?"

"Everyone misses you, but they are fine. Megara is as beautiful as ever, Hercules," Chiron said. "She is waiting for you to finish this last labor. When it is over, you can start a new life together."

Hercules smiled. "I can hardly wait."

Just then, Diogenes joined the group. He had a somber expression on his face.

"Is there bad news, Diogenes?" Hercules asked.

Diogenes looked sadly at the hero. "The king has decided on your last task. Upon finishing the assignment, you will have earned your freedom. But for your twelfth labor, you are hereby ordered to...to..."

"To what?" Hercules asked.

"Hercules, for your last labor, you must descend to the Underworld. You must go to Tartarus, the land of the dead, and bring back Cerberos, Hades' guard dog."

Hercules and his friends fell silent.

"But...how?" Hercules asked in amazement. "How can a living mortal go the Underworld?"

The Adventures of Hercules

"There is only one way," Chiron answered. "To go to the Underworld, you must *die* first."

Hercules and Chiron fasted and prayed for five days. They hoped the gods would help Hercules through his last and most terrifying labor. Hera had chosen well. It would take every ounce of Hercules' strength to come out of the Underworld alive.

When the prayers were finished, Chiron led Hercules to the mouth of a dark, deserted cave.

"Legends say this cave leads down to the Underworld," Chiron said. "No living person has gone down into the cave and returned."

Hercules embraced Chiron. "Wish me luck, my friend. I'm sure we'll see each other again. I just hope it's on this side, in the land of the living."

Without turning back, Hercules stepped into the cool, shadowy cave and began the long journey down into the bowels of the earth.

For the first few miles, the cave was fairly large and the descent was not steep. But as he got deeper into the earth, Hercules found it more difficult to move. Soon he had to bend over to avoid scraping his head on the low cave. Before long, he was on his hands and knees, pushing his club ahead of him and then crawling through the inky darkness. The temperature of the cave grew

– 114 –

warmer and warmer as the opening grew narrower.

Soon, Hercules was forced to crawl on his belly. The rocks and pebbles of the narrow tunnel crumbled and fell on his face into his eyes. With great effort, Hercules pushed his broad shoulders through the narrow passage and wormed his way through the darkness. His hands and knees were scratched and bloody. His arms were numb with fatigue, and he found it harder and harder to breathe in the stuffy, warm tunnel.

Finally, days after he began the journey, Hercules collapsed with exhaustion.

When he woke up, Hercules saw a strange glow ahead of him. He squinted down the tunnel. A face was shimmering in the darkness. It was a woman's face, beautiful and solemn, framed by copper-red hair.

"Athena?" Hercules asked.

"I will help you, Hercules," the goddess said. "You have come farther than any mortal. Zeus has allowed me to lead you to the Underworld."

Hercules smiled, filled with new confidence. He clawed at the rocks surrounding him and inched his way forward.

Athena floated down the narrow tunnel. At times Hercules got stuck, but Athena's silvery light illuminated the rocks that snagged him.

After days of crawling through the earth, Hercules saw the tunnel grow wider. Soon, Hercules was able to walk tall. Athena continued to float before him as a guide.

"How much farther, Athena?"

"Not much," she replied. "Soon you'll be in the land of the dead."

Off in the distance, Hercules heard a constant, mournful moaning.

"Those are the cries of the dead," Athena explained. "You are almost there."

The tunnel finally ended. Hercules peered out of the cave, hardly believing his eyes.

Spread out before him was a vast plain. A black river circled the entire land. Countless ghosts and hideous monsters fluttered and darted around. A black castle loomed in the center of the plain, its windows glowing with an ominous red light. A low, mournful wailing filled the air.

"Okay," Hercules said. "I'm ready for Cerberos." He looked to Athena for courage, but her image had disappeared.

There was only one way down, and Hercules carefully took the path to the banks of the black river. A low, flat boat floated across the river toward him. As the boat came to rest on the riverbank, Hercules stepped on board.

"You!" gasped the old, toothless boatman.

"Hercules, you…you are still alive!"

"Yes, I'm looking for Hades," Hercules said.

The frightened boatman grabbed his paddles. The light boat, made to carry lifeless spirits across the river, bobbed and rocked under Hercules' weight. The ferryman struggled to push it across the black water.

"No living mortal has ever crossed the river Styx," he muttered anxiously.

As they approached the opposite bank, Hercules felt his heart pound. Thousands of ghosts floated above them. They moaned and wailed pitifully.

Suddenly, Athena appeared in the mist. "These are the lost souls," she said. "They suffer. They are paying for all of the evil they did when they were alive. The spirits of the good rest in the Elysian Fields, on the other side of Hades' castle. Your sons are there."

"I hope to visit that place one day," Hercules said. "Not any time soon, of course!"

Hercules stepped from the boat. Weird ghosts with skeletal faces and withered bodies swirled around him, and Hercules tightened his grip on the handle of his club. He had to remind himself over and over that the ghosts were already dead. They could not hurt him.

As he approached the castle, Hercules saw a

huge, strange monster. It had a large head but no skin. Its body was covered with raw, bloody muscles. The monster saw Hercules and roared with pain and anger.

"The Nemean lion!" Hercules said. "It sees its skin on my back!"

"That's not the only creature you've put down here," Athena said. "Look."

Hercules turned around. The ghost of Diomedes was wrapped in chains that were attached to four black horses. The horses reared back in opposite directions, pulling on the chains. Diomedes screamed in agony.

Beyond Diomedes, Hercules saw the ghosts of Geryon and Eurytion, arguing and fighting each other with clubs.

Athena smiled at Hercules. "It's time to visit Hades, king of the Underworld," she said. "I'm sure he'll want to meet the man who has sent so many evil creatures to his kingdom."

Hercules followed Athena into the dark castle. Its dank stone walls were lit by burning torches. No guards protected the silent structure. The only sounds were the wailing of the dead outside.

The main hall ended in a large, open chamber. Two ebony black thrones were fixed in the middle of the room. There sat Hades, god of the dead, and Persephone, his bride.

Hades had a pale face and a long, thin beard, while Persephone was radiant and beautiful. She blushed and smiled at the sight of Hercules. Hades' lips curled up in a smile.

"Hercules," he greeted. "I heard you would be paying us a visit."

Hercules bowed at the god's feet. "Thank you for letting me come," he said. "It is an honor to be the first living mortal to visit your kingdom."

"It is our pleasure," Hades said in a mocking tone. "I'm sure you will come back and serve *me* in due time."

"Hercules, what can we do for you?" Persephone asked kindly.

"Your Highness, I need to borrow your guard dog, Cerberos."

"Absolutely not!" Hades shouted. His voice echoed off the castle walls. "I won't allow you to remove Cerberos from the Underworld. Cerberos keeps the spirits of the dead at bay. Some try to slip through the gates of the Underworld and cross back to the land of the living. Cerberos keeps them down here where they belong."

Hercules smiled feebly and tried to reason with Hades. "I promise to return him. I will not harm him. That you can be sure of."

Hades stood defiantly and stared Hercules down. "There is only one way you can take

Cerberos. You will have to fight me…and win!"

Hercules was stunned. How could he fight a god? For a split second, he considered turning back without Cerberos. But his conscience would not let him go.

"I'll do it," he said meekly, and raised his trusty club.

Hades laughed and shot three blazing fireballs at Hercules, who swung his club, swatting each one away. Hades continued blasting one fireball after another. They sizzled and exploded as Hercules smashed them with his club.

Hades summoned all his power and sent one last huge flame at Hercules, but the hero knocked it back with his club. The fireball zoomed across the room toward Persephone. Panicking, Hades jumped in front of the blaze. It burned white hot and then died.

"Enough!" the god raged, smoke billowing from his black tunic. "You may take Cerberos. But only if you can catch him without hurting him with your infernal club."

Hercules bowed to the gods and immediately left to look for Cerberos. He followed the dog's barks and soon located it in a dank, miserable corner of Tartarus.

The guard dog was as large as a bear. Its body looked like a dog's, but it had the long, knobby

tail of a crocodile. On its neck were three growling, snapping heads. Each head had a set of sharp
yellow teeth, which it bared at Hercules.

Hercules swallowed hard and walked up to
the dog. It immediately lurched forward and
snapped at Hercules' face. Hercules shrank back
cautiously.

He approached the beast again. This time, he
threw his club over Cerberos' head. The dog
chased after it. As soon as Cerberos' back was
turned, Hercules lunged at the three-headed dog.
He grabbed hold of the beast's stomach and lifted
the animal off the ground.

Cerberos struggled angrily for several minutes,
but Hercules held on tight. Despite the dog's
growls and grunts, Hercules would not release his
hold. Defeated, Cerberos panted quietly and followed Hercules back to the land of the living.

CHAPTER EIGHTEEN

King Eurystheus sat on his throne, terrified.

Hercules had entered the palace for the last time. On his heels was Cerberos, Hades' three-headed dog. Cerberos sniffed the king's feet and lashed his crocodile tail back and forth.

Diogenes kept far back against the door.

"Hercules, you've done your last labor," Eurystheus said, trembling. "Congratulations. Now get this dog out of here!"

"I have completed all twelve tasks. I am free now," Hercules said happily.

"Yes," Eurystheus hissed, staring at Cerberos.

"Well, then I bid you farewell." Hercules bowed and turned to leave.

"Wait!" Eurystheus begged. "You can't leave this beast here!"

"Oh, you don't want to keep him?" Hercules joked.

"No!" Eurystheus screamed.

Cerberos threw back his three heads and barked ferociously.

"All right then. Farewell!" Hercules said, and strode out of the throne room. Cerberos trailed behind him faithfully.

Outside the palace, Hercules' friends gleefully gathered around their hero. For the first time in years, Hercules' heart was light. His family waited for him back in Thebes. King Creon was eager for him to resume his place in the army.

But wherever the road would take him next, whatever challenge lay in store, Hercules was ready. He had defeated Hera again. Finally, he was free.